Edward Henry Ralph Tatham

John Sobieski

Edward Henry Ralph Tatham

John Sobieski

ISBN/EAN: 9783742861313

Manufactured in Europe, USA, Canada, Australia, Japa

Cover: Foto ©Andreas Hilbeck / pixelio.de

Manufactured and distributed by brebook publishing software
(www.brebook.com)

Edward Henry Ralph Tatham

John Sobieski

JOHN SOBIESKI.

LOTHIAN PRIZE ESSAY

FOR

1881.

BY

EDWARD H. R. TATHAM, B.A.

BRASENOSE COLLEGE.

> " Non perchè re sei tu, si grande sei,
>   Ma per te cresce e in maggior pregio sale
>   La maesta regale."
>
> VINCENZIO DA FILICAIA, *Canzone.*

OXFORD:

A. THOMAS SHRIMPTON & SON, BROAD STREET.

LONDON: SIMPKIN, MARSHALL, & CO.

1881.

JOHN SOBIESKI.

THE Kingdom or Republic of Poland has always seemed a strange phenomenon in European history, partly from the aboriginal character of its population, and partly from its exceptional constitution. The ancient Sarmatians, who occupied the same territory, had no share in the old Roman civilisation, but rather, by their constant irruptions upon the empire, were mainly instrumental in its downfall. Christianity was introduced in the tenth century; but, until recent times, no other civilising force has ever effected a permanent conquest of the country. During the eight following centuries the Poles, surrounded by enemies—on the north and east by more barbarous tribes, on the south and west by a superior civilisation—were exclusively confined to the defensive; and so missed those humanising influences to which a conquering nation has so often had to submit. As late as the eighteenth century they might truly be called the lineal descendants in race, in character, and almost in habits, of the hunters and shepherds of the ancient North. Throughout their history there were two great classes in the State; the so-called noble class—the heirs of the savage in their desire for equality, and of the nomad in their love of freedom—and the peasant class—the descendants of captives taken in war—whose lives and properties were at the absolute disposal of their masters. Only in the western portion of the kingdom was there a burgher class, and this was on the same¹ political footing with the serfs. The union of two great evils arising from such a system—licence and servitude—made the Polish constitution as disastrous as it was unique. Poland thus differed so widely, both socially and politically, from every other European state, that it would be impossible to examine any important period of her

Strangeness of Polish history.

Aboriginal character of the Poles,

Seen in their social system.

---

¹ The burghers, however, were under a separate civil jurisdiction. A tribunal for administering this foreign or Teutonic law was established in 1347 in six principal towns.

A 2

history without explaining alike her position in Europe and some of her internal peculiarities.

Although considerably[1] larger than France, Poland took scarcely any part in the general history of Europe before the end of the *European position of Poland,* sixteenth century. Once only, just before the taking of Constantinople, we find her with Hungary striving to check the advance of the Turks, when she lost in battle her king Wladislas VI. (1444). As she was the north-eastern outpost of the Church, the Popes took care that she should *At first inconsider-able,* always be remarkable for her submission to the Holy See. But it was beyond their power to check the turbulence of the nobles or to instil any love for a higher civilisation. During the sixteenth century, chiefly through the enterprise of foreigners, commerce made rapid advances in the country. English and Italian merchants, favoured by treaties between the king and queen Elizabeth, settled in the prosperous town of Dantzic, and spread a moderate knowledge of Poland in western countries. That this knowledge was only moderate may be judged from a valuable geographical work[2] published in London early in the seventeenth century, in which we are told that the Lithuanians still worshipped idols, and that in another province they had not learned the use of the plough. The reformed doctrines were widely disseminated before the year 1600; but their progress was checked by the activity of the Jesuits. The Papal *Owing to exclusiveness,* Nuncio of that time[3] complains of the exclusiveness of the Poles and their distrust of foreign nations. They used commonly to boast that alliances were of no service to them, for, if the country were conquered, they could, like their ancestors, recover in winter what they had lost in summer. Yet very early in their history they had lost the rich province of Prussia[4] by neglect and mis-government. When, in 1573, they allied themselves with France by electing as their king Henry of Valois, they bound him by such a crowd of onerous restrictions that he fled the country in disgust at their wild and barbarous freedom. During the next three quarters *Anarchy,* of a century (1573–1648), under three princes of conspicuous ability, Poland began to rank among the second-rate powers of Europe; but her internal condition was all the while frightful. Unceasing struggles between the greater

[1] Poland in the seventeenth century measured 2600 miles in circumference, while France measured only 2040.

[2] *Cosmography,* by Peter Heylin, published in 1648, reprinted from his *Microcosmus,* published in 1621.

[3] *Relatione di Polonia* (1598), quoted by Ranke (App. No. 66 to his *History of the Popes*). The same Nuncio says the Poles confessed to him that they preferred a weak monarch to an able one.

[4] The whole of the country called Prussia once belonged to Poland. Part of it, after being lost in the eleventh century, eventually came into the hands of the Elector of Brandenburg, who acknowledged the nominal suzerainty of Poland; the other part—Polish Prussia—was not lost till the eighteenth century.

and lesser nobility, and the cruel oppression of the peasants by
both alike, distracted the kingdom. Then followed
And foreign wars, thirty years of desolating war, in which the country
was several times on the brink of final subjugation
by a foreign invader. The Poles themselves attributed their
survival to God alone[1], who had preserved them to form a
barrier against the Turks.

At the close of this period, instead of finding Poland exhausted
almost to death, we see her occupying the proud position of the
Then sud- saviour of Europe. At a most critical moment, when
denly most the last great wave of barbarian invasion was rolling
prominent, over Europe, and seemed likely to overwhelm the
ancient empire of the Hapsburgs, this little republic stood firmly
in the gap, and became the bulwark of Christendom against the
infidel. Nay more, by her own sacrifices no less than by her opportune intervention, she was the main instrument in setting the final
Owing to limit to the Ottoman advance. This extraordinary
John Sobieski. result is to be ascribed almost solely to the personal
character and exploits of her patriot king, John Sobieski. Rising
to the throne by his personal merits alone in spite of the most
malignant envy, he was the first native king unconnected with the
old royal line. It may be said that his life from his early man-
hood is at no time the history of a private man; it rather com-
His difficul- prises the whole contemporary annals of his country.
ties mainly Yet it forms the most destructive comment on her
caused by the institutions, both social and political, and on the charac-
constitution. ter of the national nobility. While we must admire a
conservative constitution which admits of the supremacy of the
best man, we cannot but deplore those faults in its working which
had the effect of nullifying his authority. In Poland there was
neither a republic nor a monarchy, but the sovereignty of one
man under the control of an unrestrained class, which mistook
licence for freedom. In order to understand the position of
Sobieski and the difficulties with which he had to contend, a short
account of the Polish constitution is indispensable.

The authority of the king was originally absolute, but in a
nation of fierce warriors he was easily controlled by armed as-
Monarchy semblies of his subjects. His consulting them, though
generally at first only a mark of favour, was soon looked upon as
becomes a right; and in course of time they even claimed the
elective. disposal of his dignity. Two great dynasties suc-
cessively reigned in Poland. During the first, founded by Piast,
a native Pole (850–1386), the dignity was hereditary; during the
second, that of Jagellon (1386–1573), though in practice

---

[1] See Dr. South's letter to Dr. Edward Pococke, Hebrew lecturer at Oxford,
describing his travels in Poland. (p 71.) He mentions that he had heard them make
this remark: and it is curious that his letter bears date Dec. 16th, 1677—six years
before the relief of Vienna.

hereditary, it was in theory elective. After the latter period the
whole nobility met in arms to elect a king, and, though
Election of the king. a relation of the old line was preferred, he was considered to have no claim. This assembling of the
Pospolite, as it was called, was in an emergency the prerogative of
the king, and during an interregnum of the Primate, the Archbishop of Guesna, who acted as interrex. The election was not
legal unless it was unanimous ; and when this was accomplished,
seldom without violence, the republic imposed upon the new
monarch a contract styled "pacta conventa," the conditions of
which he swore faithfully to observe. His privileges
His privileges. were few. He always presided in the national assembly, and he might if he chose command[1] the army. But his
most important function was the appointment of officers of state.
These are said to have amounted in all branches to the astounding
number of 20,000; but only the most important, about 140,
The Senate, composed the Senate, which was the middle estate of
the realm and the real executive.

Besides the bishops there were three great orders in the
administration, of which only the first two had seats in the
How composed. Senate. These were the palatines, the castellans, and
starosts. Each palatine, like a Norman baron, was the
military commander and supreme judge in his province or
palatinate ; he was also its recognised political head. The
castellans were his deputies, who discharged the same functions in
a more confined area. The starosts were inferior magistrates, with
military and judicial duties, whose chief privilege was the high
value of their benefices. There were twelve great
The officers of state. dignitaries who were entrusted with the higher executive,—six for the kingdom of Poland, viz., the Grand
Marshal, the Grand General,[2] the Second General, the Chancellor, the
Vice-Chancellor, and the Grand Treasurer, and six parallel officers
for the Grand Duchy of Lithuania. The latter, when incorporated
with Poland in 1386, had insisted on a distinct administration ;
but the arrangement proved most unfortunate, for the Polish
magnate had no authority over his Lithuanian compeer. In the
army, as in the administration, they might act quite independently
of each other, and the very equality made a collision inevitable.
Over the Senate as a whole the king had no real power, but the
Diet exercised a rigid supervision.

This body—the third estate of the realm—had originally been
composed of the whole adult nobility. So jealous
The Diet. were the Poles of their privileges that it was not till

---

[1] This is denied by Salvandy, *Histoire du Roi Jean Sobieski,* vol. ii. p. 52, ed.
1876, though he has elsewhere admitted it by implication (vol. i. p. 402-3).
[2] The generals had no seat in the Senate by virtue of their office, but the king
always made them palatines or castellans. DALEYRAC, *Polish Manuscripts or Secret
History of the reign of John Sobieski,* ch. i. p. 9.

1466—two hundred years after the foundation of the House of Commons—that they consented to form a representative system. A Diet of 400 deputies met every two years, and was liable to be *Its depend-* summoned on extraordinary occasions. The members *ence upon the* of this assembly were absolutely without discretionary *nobility.* powers. They were elected in the dietines or provincial assemblies, and received minute instructions as to their course of action. After the dissolution of the Diet they had to appear again before their constituents and give an account of their stewardship. Those who had offended found their lives in peril. Thus the Diet took its stamp from the prevailing temper of the nobility, and, as this was almost always quarrelsome, the place of meeting often resounded with the clang of sabres. Dur-*Results of this* ing the period which we shall have to consider, this *dependence.* dependence will explain the constant neglect of proper means for the national defence. The cavalry of the nobles—the flower of the troops—displayed all the disadvantages, and none of the merits, of a standing army. They were always under arms, and ready to use them in any feud; but they could not brook strict discipline, and as they grew more luxurious their disinclina-tion[1] to a long campaign was duly reflected in the ranks of the Diet. The national haughtiness found its vent in intestine strife.

A most disastrous provision made it necessary for every *The veto.* resolution of the Diet to be unanimous. Any deputy might, without reason assigned, pronounce his veto upon the subject under discussion; nay, more, by a refinement of this privilege,[2] he might by withdrawing declare the Diet dissolved, and until he was induced or compelled to return public business was suspended. This power, though very ancient, was not exercised till 1652, but was afterwards repeated with increasing frequency. It would once have been dangerous for an individual to defy the mass, but when the republic was in a state of anarchy it was easy to find supporters, and the gold of France or Austria often proved a powerful incentive. Another mode of *Obstruction.* obstruction was called drawing out the Diet, which could not[3] sit for more than six weeks. This consisted in the proposal and tedious discussion of irrelevant matter, until the day of dissolution arrived. In this state of things a resort to force was very common, and the public streets were often the scenes of a sanguinary fray.

When the Diet was not sitting, the Senate, with the king as its president, was responsible for the government. But if the nobles were dissatisfied with their measures, or if the veto had hopelessly *Confedera-* clogged the wheels of state, recourse was had to an *tions.* extraordinary assembly called a "confederation." This

---

[1] DALEYRAC, ch. i. p. 34.
[2] The first was simply "veto," the second "veto, sisto activitatem."
[3] They were always prolonged, however, when public business was pressing.

was formed sometimes to resist, sometimes to enforce the established law; and in the latter case it often took the shape of a "convocation," which exactly resembled the Diet except that the veto was inadmissible. *Convocations.* The Poles were always more happy in organising anarchy than in organising their institutions. Of course, the authority of a confederation depended upon the number and weight of its adherents; and it frequently happened that several of these bodies were sitting at the same time. We sometimes find in Polish history the Senate at variance with the Diet, the Diet with the king, the king with the grandees, the greater with the lesser nobles, and the whole nobility with their armed serfs. Among *Strife among the nobles— how caused.* the nobles religious inequality was the principal cause of dissension. Although none but Catholics could hold offices of state, a large number of the poorer nobles were "Dissidents," and belonged to the Greek or Protestant persuasion. They were thus naturally jealous of the official families; for, though all were theoretically equal, the differences of wealth and prestige tended to divide them into three classes: first, a few *Their three main classes.* princely families who owned whole provinces and aspired to the posts of the supreme executive; secondly, the average gentry, who scrambled for the lesser offices, or were indignant at their religious disabilities; and thirdly, the poorer freemen, who made up for their lack of power by a spirit of captious disaffection. In stormy times the confusion was increased by half the middle gentry taking part with the grandees and half with the freemen.

From the highest of these classes was sprung John Sobieski. He belonged to that group of families, whose ancestral device was the *Ancestry of John Sobieski.* Buckler—the most illustrious of the rude Polish coats of arms. Far back in the mist of ages are placed the exploits of Janik—the Polish Hercules—the founder of his house. His immediate ancestors had gained less doubtful laurels. His grandfather, Mark Sobieski, palatine of Lublin, had so great a military reputation that King Stephen Bathori (1575–1586) was wont to say that he would not fear to entrust to his single arm the defence of the fortunes of Poland. His father, James Sobieski, was not only an able general, but a man of cultivated mind, and of some diplomatic skill. To him belonged the real credit of the famous victory of Kotzim in 1621 over a vast host of Turks and Tartars, although the nominal commander of the Poles was the young Prince Wladislas, son of Sigismund III. His success in negotiating the treaty that followed was so conspicuous that he was afterwards sent on several foreign embassies to the Western Powers. Such eminence in peace as in war doubtless procured for him the post of castellan of Cracow[1]—the first secular

---

[1] This castellan ranked even above all the palatines, and headed the Pospolite. The story is that in an important battle the palatine of Cracow ran away, while the castellan stood his ground, and their rank was thus reversed. (COYER, *Histoire de Sobieski*, p. 69, 8vo ed.)

senator of Poland, inferior only to the archbishop of Guesna. He
had also been four times elected Marshal of the Diet—an office
resembling that of Speaker of the House of Commons. In or
about 1620 he married Theophila Danilowiczowna, grand-daughter[1]
of the famous Zolkiewski. That heroic general, after taking Moscow
(1610), and carrying off to Poland the Czar Basil VI., met his death
(October 5th, 1620) at Kobylta on the Dniester, with a band of
8,000 men, at the hands of 70,000[2] Turks and Tartars. Thus on
both sides the ancestors of Sobieski were worthy of his subsequent
fame. The circumstances of his birth are romantic ;
Birth. but they rest on no less an authority than a manuscript
in his own hand. On the 17th of June, 1624,[3] his father's castle
of Zloçkow in the palatinate of Red Russia[4] was visited by a storm
of unprecedented violence. The old mansion, which stood exposed
on the bare summit of a vast "mohila" or Slavonic tumulus, was
shaken to its foundations, and some of the attendants were
rendered deaf for life. Amid the raging of the elements was born
John Sobieski, in the presence of the widow of the conqueror of
Moscow ; and the respect for prodigies,[5] which distinguishes the
Poles above all other modern nations, must have marked him out
in their eyes for an exceptional career. Yet his youth was singu-
larly peaceful. Except for the war against Gustavus Adolphus,
which was terminated by the peace of Altmark (September 15th,
1629), and an incursion of the Tartars (1636), successfully re-
pelled by Wladislas VII., Poland enjoyed from the time of his
birth an unexampled respite of more than twenty years.

During this period John and his elder brother Mark were
enjoying all the benefits of a careful education. Their father
chiefly resided at his princely estate of Zolkiew, which
Education. had come to him through his wife—a domain as large
as some of our English counties, and embracing a hundred and
fifty villages. He had engaged as their tutor the learned Stanislas
Orchowski ; but he himself superintended their more important
studies. The treatise which he has left upon education is alone
enough to show how well the task must have been performed.

---

[1] The Abbé Coyer makes her his daughter ; but he is wrong. The daughter of
Zolkiewski married into the family of Danilowicz, and was the mother of Theophila.
(SALVANDY, vol. i. 145 -147.)

[2] The disparity is said to have been much greater, but it is necessary to bear in
mind throughout the life of Sobieski that the numbers of the combatants are un-
certain, owing to the Polish habit of exaggeration.

[3] Most historians (and Salvandy in his first edition, 1827) follow Coyer in giving
the date 1629. Salvandy gives no reason for the change in his later editions ; but
Sobieski must have been older than fourteen when he travelled in France ; and it
appears that his manuscript favours the earlier date. Coyer is most inaccurate until
the campaign of Podhaic, where his original authorities begin, and is untrustworthy
afterwards.

[4] Russia, properly so-called, was at this time a province of Poland. The empire
of the Czars was termed Muscovy.

[5] Sobieski himself was not free from this feeling. See the collection of his
letters by M. le Comte Plater (Letter xvii.).

Besides instructing them in several languages he imparted to them his own skill in music, painting, and the other fine arts; and they had the rare advantage of a home in which to the barbaric splendour of a Polish noble were added some of the refined tastes of an Italian court. Ardent and robust by nature, John early distinguished himself by his activity in hunting, and in the use of the small sword ; and the traditions of his family soon taught him against whom his strength was to be employed. The inscription[1] on his great grandfather's tomb in the neighbouring Dominican chapel, erected by his mother, aroused in his mind what may be called his life-purpose—to curb at all hazards the advance of the Turkish power.

At length in 1643 the castellan sent his two sons to travel in the West. Their longest stay was made in France—at that time *His travels.* closely united to Poland by the marriage of Wladislas with a French princess[2]—but they also visited England[3] and Italy. At Paris they frequented the salon of the Duchesse de Longueville, sister of the great Condé; and it was here that an intimacy sprang up between John Sobieski and the French general, who, though only three years his senior, was already crowned with the laurels of Rocroi. The prince procured for his friend the honour of a commission in the king's Grands Mousquetaires, and continued in correspondence with him during the remainder of his life. Quitting France before the disturbances of the Fronde, the brothers took the measure of the Ottoman power at Constantinople, and were preparing to pass into Asia, when news arrived which called them home to defend not only their country but their own fireside. It was to the effect that the Cossack serfs had revolted, and were carrying all before them.

Of the grinding oppression under which the serf class laboured we have already spoken. Some efforts had been made by Casimir *Cossack revolt* the Great (1347) to give them a legal footing in the *caused by the* state ; and he had even succeeded so far as to provide *oppression of* that the murderer of a serf should pay a fine of ten *the serfs.* marks.[4] But his regulations were soon broken, and the condition of the peasants in the outlying districts became more hopeless than before. The situation of the Cossacks was peculiar. *The Cossacks.* Inhabiting a wild though fertile country on the borders of Poland and Muscovy called the Ukraine (Slavonic for "borderland," exactly the French "marche"), they had long

---

[1] It was part of Dido's dying speech :
        "Exoriare aliquis nostris ex ossibus ultor."
Theophila is said to have shown her sons the hero's shield while repeating the Spartan injunction "with it or upon it."

[2] Louise de Nevers. The Sobieskis were in France when the embassy came to fetch her. She also married Casimir, the next king.

[3] We find only the bare statement that they visited England (Salvandy ; Palmer, *Memoirs of John Sobieski*). It is possible the civil war may have deterred them.

[4] Of these only five were paid to the family of the murdered man, the other five going to his lord.

retained their independence, and had only been incorporated in the kingdom by the wise measures of Stephen Bathori (1582). Origi-
Under Stephen Bathori. nally deserters from the armies of the republic, they had betaken themselves to the almost inaccessible isles of the Borysthenes, where they led a life of plunder in defiance of their neighbours. Their piratical skiffs were an object of terror even to the dwellers on the Golden Horn. Bathori did all that lay in his power to conciliate a people who, in spite of their savage habits, were noted for their fidelity. He gave them the city of Tretchimirow in Kiowia, and formed them into regiments, for the defence of Poland against the Tartars. They were granted the power of electing their own hetman, or Grand General, who, on doing homage to the king, received as the symbols of his office a flag, a horsetail, a staff, and a looking-glass. James Sobieski in his historical work [1] notices the value to a retreating Polish army of their waggon-camps, which they called "Tabora," [2] and which they seem to have drawn up after the fashion of a Dutch "laager." Unfortunately their independence was confined to the period of military service. The Ukraine, like other parts of the kingdom of Poland, was divided into estates of crown land, which, like fiefs,[3] were held by the nobles on condition of furnishing the state with troops. But this condition was seldom fulfilled even in Great Poland, and never in a distant province, such as the Ukraine, where all the nobles were absentees.

There was thus no tie except that of gratitude for their honourable position in war to bind the Cossacks to Poland; and this was
Their grievances. soon broken by the outrageous rapacity of the Jewish stewards to whom the nobles entrusted their lands. Complaints were lodged in the Diet by the Cossack chiefs, who claimed to send thither their own representatives; but the nobles, whose love of domination was as strong as their love of liberty, turned a deaf ear; and Wladislas VII., seeing the fatal tendency of this policy, had the hardihood to remind the Cossacks that they still possessed their sabres.[4] At length, in 1648, a dastardly outrage by a steward on Bogdan Chmielnicki, one of their chiefs, forced them to follow this hint; and electing the injured man as their hetman, they poured into Poland with the
Success of their revolt. Tartars as their allies. Bogdan was an experienced soldier. He completely defeated Potoski, the Grand General of Poland, at Korsun (May 26th, 1648); and numbers of disaffected Poles—Arian nobles, Calvinistic burghers,

---

[1] *Commentariorum Chotimensis belli libri tres.* CRACOW, 1646.
[2] These were not broken during a march, differing in this from the laager. See DALEYRAC, ch. i. p. 24.
[3] It was not a feudal tenure, however, for the nobles did not acknowledge any vassalage to the king. It was merely a bargain.—DALEYRAC, ch. i. p. 23.
[4] Dyer (*Modern Europe*, vol. iii. p. 42, ed. 1864) gives no authority for his extraordinary statement that Wladislas entered into an elaborate conspiracy with the Cossacks against his own kingdom. Nothing could be more foreign to his character.

outlawed serfs—at once flocked to his standard. Six days before *Death of* this disaster Wladislas VII. expired at Warsaw; and *Wladislas* his death at this moment blighted the hopes of the *VII.* moderate party. James Sobieski, who had done all he could to save Bogdan from oppression, had died in March (1648) when the king was on the point of naming him the representative of Poland at the congress in Westphalia. The nobility in general were bent on revenge. Assembling their forces in haste, they *Danger of* suffered an ignominious defeat at Pilawiecz (September *Poland.* 23rd); and Poland was left exposed to the Cossacks.

Madame Sobieska, with her two daughters, and many others of the nobility, took refuge within the walls of Zamosç, and was soon joined by her sons, who had evaded without difficulty the undisciplined besiegers.

At this crisis the nobles assembled at Warsaw to elect a king. They chose (November 20th) Cardinal John Casimir, *Election* brother of the late king, who put off the purple to *of John* assume the crown. The new prince saw the necessity *Casimir.* of conciliation, and had the courage, in spite of the opposition of the nobles, to open a negotiation with the rebels. Bogdan, who had been deserted by the Tartars, was not disinclined for peace, and, in order to show his respect for the king, retired *His peace* thirty leagues from Zamosç. But the treachery of the *violated by the* nobles frustrated the intentions of their sovereign. *nobles.* Jeremiah Wiesnowiesçki, the harsh oppressor of the serfs, fell suddenly upon the unsuspecting Cossacks, and routed them with great slaughter. After this the war broke out afresh. Bogdan sought and obtained the alliance of Isla, khan of the Crim Tartars, and in an engagement at Zbaraz, in Vollhynia (June 30th, 1649) he gained another great victory. At this news the king hastened to join the remnants of the defeated army, and was *Sobieski* accompanied by John Sobieski in command of a select *joins the* troop. The young noble had been prevented taking *army,* part in the events of the past six months by a wound which he had received in a duel with one of the family of Paz, the most powerful clan in Lithuania; and he afterwards had cause to regret the quarrel. His presence with the king at this juncture was destined to be of some importance. No sooner had Casimir assembled the discomfited Poles, than half his available force, terrified at the enemy's numbers, insisted on retreat, and proceeded *And quells a* to put their threat into execution. Sobieski galloped *mutiny.* into their midst, and, exerting that native eloquence of which he possessed no common share, succeeded in restoring them to their allegiance. His efforts were rewarded by the starosty of Javarow—a military post which had been previously held by his father and by the great Zolkiewski. One of the immediate results of the bold front now presented by the Poles, was the conclusion of the peace of Zborow (August 18th), in which the Cossack chief displayed remarkable moderation.

Peace of Zborow. He consented to do homage to the king and to forego his just demands for vengeance upon his oppressors, on condition that all his adherents should receive a free pardon.

But the Polish nobility were incapable of learning any lesson *Broken by the Poles. June 30th, 1651.* from their recent reverses. War was again declared by the Diet in 1650; and the next year Bogdan was defeated by Casimir at Berestezko, owing principally to the desertion of the Tartars. In this battle, John Sobieski received a wound in his head, from the effects of which he suffered constantly until his death. A transitory peace which followed this success was again broken by the Poles, who attacked Bogdan's son Timothy at Batowitz (June 2nd, 1652), but were surrounded and annihilated. The prisoners, among whom was Mark Sobieski,[1] *Death of Mark Sobieski.* were all massacred after the battle by the Tartar khan. Another duel wound fortunately prevented John from being among the victims. But he had the pain of seeing that his folly had made his mother despair of the name of Sobieski. Overwhelmed with grief at the loss of her favourite son, and auguring ill from the headstrong passions of John, she quitted Poland and took refuge in Italy.

The Cossack war, which had now lasted with little intermission for four years, demands considerable attention. It throws a lurid *Lessons of the Cossack War.* light on the vices of the Polish constitution, and its bitter lessons cannot have been lost upon a thoughtful mind like that of John Sobieski. By oppression the Polish nobility had converted faithful subjects into deadly foes; and their pride and treachery contrast most unfavourably with the moderation of the Cossack chief. Although we have little information about this period of Sobieski's life, his ardent temper makes it probable that he joined at first with the most uncompromising of the nobles. But their independence of the regal authority, their disregard for treaties with the serf class, and, above all, their unprecedented employment of the fatal veto (1652), must have soon convinced him that the discipline of self-restraint was the only means left to save his country. Hereafter we shall see him nobly practising this lesson under the most fearful provocation.

At this period (1654) Poland was distracted by anarchy at home, and in the next six years she suffered all the usual consequences of *Anarchy.* civil strife. Henceforward the Cossack war loses its character of a struggle between the republic and her rebellious subjects. Its natural result was to draw into the contest those neighbouring nations who might hope to gain advantage from

---

[1] Coyer makes Mark Sobieski die four years earlier, but his account of the Cossack war is so confused, that it is difficult to tell to what events he refers.

the distracted state of Poland. Bogdan, despairing of concluding
The Cossacks any definitive peace without foreign aid, persuaded the
call in Mus- Czar Alexis to declare war against Poland, and, on the
covy. frivolous pretext that his titles had not received due
respect, that monarch invaded Lithuania and took Smolensko
(Sept. 10th, 1654).

But a greater enemy was arising in the north; Charles X. of
Sweden, the "Pyrrhus of the North," succeeding to the throne on
War with the abdication of Christina in June 1654, had set his
Sweden. mind on the conquest of Poland. The Polish vice-
chancellor, Radzejowski, who had been expelled from
the kingdom by Casimir on some private quarrel, took care that
Charles should be well acquainted with the weakness to which his
country had been reduced. He gave the welcome advice that no
apology which Casimir might make as to his assumption of the
title of king of Sweden [1] should receive any attention. The king of
Poland was anxious to send Sobieski to Stockholm to avert the
impending storm; but he declined the hopeless mission. Charles
eagerly took advantage of the anarchy caused by the Russian war,
and invaded Pomerania and Great Poland in August, 1655. He
gained an easy victory over the divided forces of the republic, and
entered Warsaw at the end of the month. Cracow surrendered
early in October, and, as Casimir had fled into Silesia, the whole
Charles X. country lay at his feet. Surrounded by such a host of
conquers enemies, the nobles seemed to have no choice but to
Poland, offer the crown to Charles X.; and the standing army,
called Quartians,[2] among whom Sobieski commanded a troop, took
But alienates the oath to the king of Sweden. But Charles was not
it. inclined to keep faith with a people whom he had conquered in three months. Contrary to his express promises
hereditary monarchy was proclaimed, heavy contributions were
levied, and the Catholics were openly persecuted by the Swedes.
The national spirit was deeply wounded by the haughty demeanour
Resumption of the conquerors. During the absence of Charles in
of the war. Prussia, a confederation was formed in the palatinate of
Beltz under the auspices of the absent Casimir, to which
Sobieski attached himself, and with him the able generals Lubomirski and Czarniecki. When Charles returned he found that he had
the greater part of Poland to re-conquer. In conveying his army
Successes of through the marshes of Little Poland, he was blocked
Sobieski. up between the Vistula and the San by Sobieski's
cavalry, and was only extricated by the prompt arrival
of reinforcements. Soon after, while he was superintending the

---

[1] He was descended from the elder branch of the house of Vasa—that of his grandfather, John III. of Sweden. His father, Sigismund III. of Poland, had by his
Polish sympathies and Catholic education, alienated the affections of the Swedes.
[2] The Polish regular army was so called because a fourth of the royal revenues was
employed to maintain them. SALVANDY, i. p. 404.

siege of Dantzic, Casimir and the valiant Czarniecki recaptured Warsaw; but they lost it again on his return after a battle of three days, in which Sobieski, who commanded a troop of Tartars' trained by himself, performed prodigies of valour. But other nations had looked on with jealousy at the brilliant career of the king of Sweden. The Czar, resenting the manner in which he had been baulked of his prey, declared war against Sweden; and the emperor Ferdinand III., just before his death (May 30th, 1657), concluded an offensive

Charles attempts a partition, and defensive alliance with the king of Poland. Meanwhile Charles was using all his efforts to carry out a scheme for the partition of Poland between himself, the Czar, the Great Elector of Brandenburg,[2] and Ragoczy, prince of Transylvania. But her time had not yet come. Almost at the same moment Denmark declared war against Charles, the Elector deserted him, and Austria prepared to send troops in support of her new ally (June, 1657).

But is obliged to retire. In July Charles evacuated Poland in all haste, and began his wonderful campaigns in Denmark. Another stroke of good fortune was the death of Bogdan Chmielnicki (August 27th), and the return of a large number of Cossacks to their allegiance.

Gradual recovery of Poland. Though sorely shaken by the terrible ordeal through which she had passed, Poland gradually recovered her independence. Treaties were concluded with the Elector, and with Prince Ragoczy, with no more serious loss than the suzerainty of ducal Prussia (1658); and two years later, shortly after the death of Charles X., a peace was signed with Sweden at Oliva (May 3rd, 1660). Casimir re-established his authority throughout

Sobieski rewarded. the kingdom; and in distributing rewards to his most faithful subjects, conferred upon Sobieski the post of Korongy, or standard-bearer of the crown.[3]

There still remained, however, the war with Muscovy. The ever-active Czar Alexis, now that he could take his own measures with

War with Muscovy. Poland, overran Lithuania, and captured Wilna, its capital. But his general, Sheremetieff, suffered a serious defeat, and shut himself up in his fortified camp at Cudnow to await the arrival of a large reinforcement of Cossacks. Sobieski was detached with a small force from the investing army to confront this new enemy. Finding them encamped on the

Victories of Sobieski at Slobodyszcza and Cudnow. heights of Slobodyszcza, he carried the position by assault, and gained a victory so complete that the Cossacks laid down their arms (Sept. 17th, 1660). He then hastened back to Cudnow, and joined in the

---

[1] Coyer, who is followed by other writers, says that Sobieski was once a hostage with the khan of the Tartars at his own request, and made him a steady friend of Poland.

[2] Frederic William, the founder of the greatness of the house of Hohenzollern.

[3] He only carried the standard in the Pospolite; his office was a high military command. Coyer makes this the reward of his quelling the mutiny at Zborow, which seems most improbable.

attack on the Muscovite camp, which was so successful that the whole army, with their ammunition and stores, fell into the hands of the Poles. Such a brilliant campaign astonished Europe. Sobieski, whose reputation was already high in his own country, was justly credited with giving her breathing time to recover from her misfortunes.

She employed it, according to her wont, in internal dissensions. It is difficult to trace the true origin of the deplorable state of

Anarchy in Poland. Poland during the next six years; but it may be attributed, in the first instance, to the foolish conduct of the queen, Louise de Nevers. Though a woman of masculine spirit, and exercising a great ascendancy over the uxorious Casimir, she was herself entirely governed by the Jesuits. They

1661. persuaded her, and through her the king, to violate that article of the *pacta conventa* by which he pledged himself not to tamper with the succession to the crown. The person for whom they designed it was her nephew, the young Duc d'Enghien, son of the great Condé. The power of French gold

1662-3. soon converted the majority of the senate. But the lesser nobles were not so easily cajoled, and they possessed a secret though powerful supporter in Lubomirski, Grand Marshal and Second General of the crown. To this main grievance was added another, which pressed heavily on the poorer nobles. Large arrears of pay were, as usual,[1] owing to the army, who accordingly formed themselves into a confederation, and demanded the diminution of the immense revenues of the clergy. This brought upon them all the thunders of the Church; and the fearful spectacle was presented of a country divided into hostile camps, in which the senate was at enmity with the diet, the clergy with the army, the larger with the lesser nobility. Sobieski and other patriotic spirits tried to strike at the root of the evil, and furnished funds from their private resources for the payment of arrears. As this did not allay the complaints of the army, the senate opened a negotiation with the malcontents from Sobieski's "court"[2] at Zolkiew, which was so far successful that the king was able to lead them

Campaign against Muscovy. against Muscovy. But the campaign, though not disastrous, was not especially fortunate; and the absence of Lubomirski, who had been kept at home by the king's suspicions, created general discontent.

On his return the king summoned Lubomirski to trial on a

Sobieski, Grand Marshal and Second General. charge of high treason. He did not appear, and was condemned to perpetual banishment and the loss of his honours and estates. His office of Grand Marshal was bestowed on Sobieski, and that of Second General on Czarniecki; but the latter dying shortly after, this post

---

[1] Daleyrac (ch. i. p. 28) represents the army as being at the mercy of the Grand Treasurer, who frequently pocketed the money.
[2] The mansion of a Polish noble was called his "court."

was also conferred on Sobieski. The appointments were most politic, for Sobieski was a great favourite with the army. His duties having kept him constantly on the Cossack frontier, he had not compromised himself with either party.

Marriage of Sobieski. These signs of the royal favour were followed by another which bound him still more to the interests of the court. On his visit to Warsaw to assume the insignia of his offices, he became enamoured of a French lady in the retinue of the queen, Mary Casimira d'Arquien, who had lately become a widow by the death of the rich Prince Zamoyski. She was daughter to the Marquis d'Arquien, captain of the guards to the Duke of Orleans, and had attended the queen from France nineteen years before. Though over thirty years of age,

His wife. she still possessed in a remarkable degree all those fascinations which usually belong to extreme youth. Dr. South, who saw her seven years later, says that even then she did not look more than twenty.[1] To these advantages she united a piquant vivacity which had a peculiar charm for Sobieski. His passion was so strong[2] that he besought the queen's consent to their immediate union. Scarcely four weeks had elapsed since the death of Zamoyski, to whom she had borne several children; but so necessary was it to conciliate the new officer that the queen gave way, and the marriage was celebrated, according to the Polish fashion, by a festival of three days. Sobieski was hereafter to receive severe punishment for this indecent haste in the conduct of his wife. In the midst of the

July, 5-7, 1665. marriage *fêtes* tidings arrived that Lubomirski, who had entered Poland with a large army, was ungenerously plundering

Rebellion of Lubomirski. his estate at Zolkiew, and carrying off his stud of horses. The proscribed general, who was a prince of the empire, had received secret support from Leopold of Austria, and was now in open rebellion.

The whole kingdom was divided against itself. The palatinates of the west, gained over by Austria, resented the predominance of France at court, and joined Lubomirski. An effort was

Sobieski tries arbitration. made by Sobieski to get the decision of the Diet on Lubomirski's claims, but the assembly was dissolved by the fatal veto, and the two armies advanced to the struggle. Contrary to the earnest advice of Sobieski, Casimir made his attack in the marshes of Montwy (July 11th, 1666), and his troops, entangled in the difficult ground, were easily de-

Peace with Lubomirski. feated. But Lubomirski was anxious to come to terms, and, having extracted a promise from Casimir that he

---

[1] But he says she was then only thirty-three, and she was certainly six years older. Louise de Nevers would not have taken away to Poland a child of five years as part of her suite.
[2] Connor (*Letters on Poland*, Letter iv.) actually represents that he was unwilling to marry her until tempted by a large dowry.

would not interfere in the succession, he waived his personal claims, and retired to Silesia, where he died six months after.

His faction, however, was not silenced. Bands of hungry soldiers, clamouring for pay, levied black-mail upon the provinces; *Invasion of the Tartars.* and the central authority seemed powerless to restrain them. At this juncture news arrived that 80,000 Tartars were plundering Volhynia, and that the Cossacks under Doroscensko were preparing to join them. The utmost consternation prevailed at Warsaw; a peace was hastily patched up with Muscovy, and efforts were made to raise fresh troops. But the treasury was empty; the republic had only 10,000 men under arms; and many of these were most imperfectly equipped. Casimir applied vainly for help at the principal European courts; Brandenburg alone sent a few companies of infantry. At this crisis Potoçki, the aged Grand General, died, and the king at once appointed the Grand Marshal to the post.

Never before had any Polish subject united in his own person these two offices. As Grand General Sobieski had absolute con-*Sobieski Grand General,* trol over military affairs, and could quarter his army where he pleased; as Grand Marshal he was at the head of the administration, received foreign ambassadors, and could inflict death without appeal. In most points, as in the *As well as Grand Marshal.* last, his power was really greater than that of the king; for although the king could confer these honours, he could not revoke them. No higher testimony could have been paid to the prudence and ability of Sobieski than the readiness with which these unusual powers were granted, and the very transitory murmurs that they provoked amongst an exceptionally jealous nobility. His rise, though fortunate at its close, had not been so rapid as to be out of proportion to his merits. The gravity of the crisis doubtless operated in his favour; and he took pains at once to relieve all suspicion by his temperate and vigorous action. His persuasive eloquence silenced the clamours for pay, and he hesitated not to drain his private coffers in raising new levies. By this means he doubled his original forces, and then *His bold plan of the campaign.* prepared to execute a grand plan for the destruction of the Tartars. Throwing his army into the fortified camp of Podhaic, a small town in Red Russia, he detached several large bodies of cavalry to act in the vicinity. These had orders on a given day, when the enemy had worn himself out by the assault, to close round the vast host and help their general to assume the offensive. To divide so small a force seemed hazardous in the extreme,[1] and the soldiers murmured openly that their lives were to be thrown away. The cool courage of Sobieski made them blush for shame. "He gave all cowards liberty to depart; as for

---

[1] A letter of Sobieski, describing this plan to his wife, who was staying in France, was shown to Condé, who had no hope of its success.

himself, he was determined to remain with all those who loved their country." The enemy appeared; and for seventeen days in succession this heroic band withstood their most determined assaults. Finally Sobieski, whose troops had suffered far less loss than they inflicted, gave the signal to his out-lying parties, and attacked the Tartars in front and rear. The battle was hotly contested; but at length victory declared for the Poles. Galga, the Tartar khan, found his troops so severely handled that he was forced to sue for peace, and concluded an alliance with the republic. Doroscensko, on the part of the Cossacks, agreed to restore to the nobles their estates in the Ukraine.

Sept. 28th-Oct. 15th, 1667.

Great victory of Podhaic.

Poland had been saved almost by a miracle; and multitudes flocked to the churches to return thanks to God. When the danger was at its height, so inert and feeble was the body-politic that Casimir had found it impossible to arm the Pospolite for the relief of their devoted general. Their gratitude was now the greater that their sacrifices had been few. When Sobieski on his return detailed in modest language the success of the campaign, and ascribed his victory to the mercy of God, the Diet rose with one accord and answered that the republic knew who had saved her, and would remember to thank him. The tidings reached his wife, who was staying with her relatives in France, just after she had borne him a son; and such was the general admiration that Louis XIV. and Henrietta Maria, the mother of Charles II., were willing to answer for the child at the font. He was named James Louis, in honour of his grandfather and his illustrious sponsor.

Gratitude of Poland.

Birth of a son.

No successes against the invader could allay the internal broils of Poland. Although Casimir had lost his queen in the spring of the year 1667, the outcry against the French influence continued unabated. On one occasion the king so far forgot himself as to exclaim, in full diet, "If you are weary of me, I am no less weary of you." At length, bowed down by domestic sorrow, tormented by scruples of conscience,[1] and disgusted at the turbulence of the nobles, he came to the resolution, which those words seemed to imply, of laying aside the crown. He took farewell of the Diet in a dignified speech, in which he asked only for six feet of earth, where his bones might rest in peace. If he had offended any, he begged them to forgive him as freely as he forgave those who had offended him. The assembly was profoundly affected; but, although Sobieski and others from motives of gratitude besought him to retain the crown, it does not appear that this was the wish of the nation. We are told that on the day after his abdication the people hardly paid him the respect

Abdication of John Casimir.

---

[1] He was tormented with remorse for marrying his brother's widow.

due to a gentleman;[1] and much ill-feeling was shown in the Diet, when the question of his pension came before it. After remaining in Poland too long for his own credit[2] he retired to France, where Louis XIV. gave him the Abbey of St. Germain. He was the last of the dynasty of Jagellon,[3] which had reigned in Poland nearly three hundred years.

The number of aspirants to the vacant throne was, as usual, considerable. *Candidates for the throne.* The Czar Alexis massed 80,000 troops on the frontier in support of the candidature of his son, but the Poles took little notice either of him or his manœuvres. The Prince of Condé was supported by Sobieski and many of the Senate, but the prejudice against a Frenchman was universal among the lesser nobles. The two candidates most in favour were Prince Charles of Lorraine, secretly supported by Austria, and Philip, Duke of Neuberg, who, though sixty years of age, was set up as the real choice alike of the King of France and the Emperor. The personal advantages of the former were far superior to those of his rival; he was young, courageous, and affable; but he had neither money nor lands, while the offers of the Duke of Neuberg were most advantageous to the state. The nobles, fully alive to the value of their votes, postponed *Disorder on the field of election.* their decision till May, 1669; and meanwhile the field of election was as usual a scene of wild confusion. A large party clamoured for the exclusion of the Prince of Condé, and, although Sobieski protested against such a measure as interfering with the freedom of the proceedings, it was carried through by the violence of its promoters. At length the tumult rose to such a height that Sobieski, as Grand-Marshal, threatened to fire upon the rioters. Order was thus partly restored; and soon the cry of a Piast! a Piast! was heard among the crowd. Sobieski might well suppose that no Piast (or native Pole) would be thought so worthy as himself to wear the crown, but perhaps he had made himself too unpopular during the election. The cry was followed by the proposal of Michael Wiesnowiesçki—a young noble barely thirty years of age, who had neither virtues, nor abilities, nor riches to recommend him to their suffrages. Yet such was the *Proclamation of King Michael.* fickle excitability of the assembly that he was chosen by acclamation; and, although he implored to be spared the honour, and even attempted to escape, he was dragged to the throne, and invested with the supreme authority.

The reign of such a king could scarcely be prosperous. Ere long the nobles had cause to regret that they had not chosen the man who of all native Poles was worthiest to hold the sceptre. Michael himself, when mounted upon the throne, could not but

[1] Connor (Letter iii.) mentions having heard this from aged Poles.
[2] He stayed till the diet of election was opened.
[3] The next king, though related to it, could hardly be said to belong to it, as he was descended from Korybuth, uncle of Jagellon.

see that he was far from being the first man in the republic. The thought wounded his pride, which was soon to become as conspicuous as his previous humility. He hated Sobieski *His hatred of Sobieski,* with a hatred the more violent that he was unable to abridge his powers. He refused the grand coach-and-six which it was the established custom for the general to present to the new sovereign.[1] He plotted with Christopher and Michael Paz, respectively chancellor and grand general of Lithuania, against the man with whom they had a long-standing *Who was* family feud.[2] But Sobieski, besides having the army at *popular with* his back, was zealously supported by the greater nobles, *the army.* and although a struggle appeared imminent the king's party forbore for a time. Efforts were made to promote a reconciliation by marrying Michael to the daughter of Sobieski's sister ;[3] but the plan was overthrown by the arrival of an ambassador from Leopold to offer him the hand of the Arch-Duchess Eleanor. The honour was too tempting for the weak-minded king; he accepted from the emperor the order of the Golden Fleece, and *Marriage of* hastily concluded the marriage without the sanction of *Michael.* the republic. Loud were the complaints against this breach of the constitution,[4] even among his own supporters, the lesser nobles. Austria had always been distrusted by the Poles, but at this moment there was a special reason for her unpopularity.

On the 2nd of September, 1669, after a most memorable defence of more than twenty years, the city and island of Candia surrendered to the Turkish fleet, commanded by the Grand *Siege of Candia.* Vizier, Ahmed Köprili. The vast designs of this able *Designs of* minister were the terror of Europe. Five years earlier *Ahmed* (1664) he had concluded with Austria a twenty years' *Köprili.* peace, on terms most favourable to the Turks ; and it was well known that he only awaited the fall of Candia to resume his schemes against Italy and the empire. That result was now achieved, a peace was concluded with Venice, and he was free to turn the Ottoman arms towards the west and north. The Marquis de St. André,[5] who had commanded in Candia, wrote into *Terror in* France that Köprili had opened the way to Rome, and *Europe at* by what he knew of that general's humour, he doubted not but he had a design to turn St. Peter's church into the Grand Signor's stables. It is even said that Pope Clement IX. died of grief at the Turkish successes. These fears were doubtless in part well founded. During the Thirty Years' War, and the

---

[1] Connor, Letter iv.
[2] Begun by his duel with one of their clan in 1648.
[3] Married to Radziwill, the Croesus of Lithuania.
[4] The king bound himself by the *pacta conventa* not to marry without the consent of the republic.
[5] See Daleyrac, chap. i. p. 39.

intestine struggles which succeeded it in many of the Christian states, the Turkish power had steadily increased. Two Grand Viziers of consummate ability, Mahommed Köprili and his son Ahmed, had strengthened the empire by numerous fortresses, had sternly quelled the frequent revolts, and had introduced a spirit of order and activity hitherto seldom seen among the Turks. If the jealousies of France and Austria were to continue, a wise vizier might well hope ere long to make a tremendous onslaught upon Christendom. It is not surprising therefore that, after the fall of Candia, the Poles should resent the Emperor's crafty aim to secure their taking up arms in his defence.

The rise of Turkey.

But the danger was nearer than they imagined. It threatened them as usual from the quarter of the Cossacks, who had never since their first revolt in 1648 preserved a real peace with Poland. They viewed with dismay the accession to the throne of a son of their former oppressor, Jeremiah Wiesnowiescki, and imagining that his first object would be to recover his lost estates, they rushed to arms. Immediately after the coronation of Michael (October, 1669) Sobieski was called to the frontiers. Acting with his usual vigour, he sowed discord in the enemy's ranks, and drove them beyond the Dniester. So unexpected were these victories that the Vice-Chancellor, writing to him in the king's name, says: "Envy itself is compelled to confess that, after God, you alone, though at the head of so small a force, have once more saved Poland." But the king and his general could not agree as to the measures to be taken with the subdued Cossacks. Sobieski was most anxious for a policy of concession. He had seen signs among them of a disposition to call in the Turks, which they had attempted to do in 1651, and he hoped to avert such a disaster. But Michael was wholly deaf to argument. Finding that the Diet was likely to declare against him, he easily procured its dissolution by the veto (April 17th); and the event which Sobieski dreaded came to pass. Doroscensko, the Cossack chief, losing all hope of justice from Poland, and persuaded by his metropolitan that he would find it at the patriarchate of the East, went to Constantinople to throw himself at the feet of the Sultan.

Revolt of the Cossacks.

Sobieski's campaign of 1670.

Michael refuses a policy of concession.

The Cossacks apply to the Porte.

Fortune seemed to play into the hands of Ahmed Köprili. The restless janissaries needed employment, and he preferred a gradual advance upon Austria to a premature declaration of war with her. Poland seemed to offer a splendid field. Proclaiming the Sultan the champion of the oppressed, he prepared a great armament against the oppressor, and created Doroscensko hospodar of the Ukraine. But his plans required time to be fully matured, and in the meanwhile he encouraged the Tartars to burst into Poland (1671).

Köprili prepares for war with Poland.

The republic was at this moment torn in pieces by the violence of the Austrian and French factions. Leopold had followed up *Austrian* his success in the marriage of his sister by surrounding *influence in* the weak Michael with creatures of his own, who used *Poland.* all their arts to persuade him that the French monarch had been guilty of bringing in the Tartars against him. Great efforts were made to include Sobieski in these accusations. His second general, Demetrius Wiesnowiesçki, the king's cousin, who had long been jealous of him, actually put Tartar captives to the torture to obtain evidence, but without success. Sobieski, though deeply indignant, contented himself with publishing a scornful manifesto, and then hastened to defend the frontiers. At the meeting of the Diet (September 20th) the deputies demanded the dismissal of the Austrian courtiers; and the primate Prazmowski vehemently accused the king of treachery to the nation, and of breaking his coronation oaths. Terrified at this attack, Michael *Michael calls* called out the Pospolite, which was devoted to his *out the Pospo-* interests; but he paid no attention to the entreaties of *lite.* Sobieski that he would use it against the invader. He could not bring himself to save his kingdom at the expense of strengthening his rival.

Sobieski determined to act without him. Equipping the regular army at his own cost, he appeared to be covering Kaminiec, the *"Miraculous* key of south-eastern Poland, but when the Tartar hordes *campaign" of* had passed into Volhynia, he marched with surprising *Sobieski.* celerity through Podolia, and cut them off from their allies, the Cossacks. Trembling for their retreat the barbarians broke up their camp, and hurried out of the country as fast as they could, while Sobieski made a triumphant progress through the Ukraine, capturing several towns which had not seen a Polish army for twenty years, and re-establishing communications with the friendly Moldavians. Europe justly termed this "the miraculous campaign;" yet it was accomplished almost solely by the strenuous exertions of the commander. His troops were in the worst possible condition, the Lithuanian army had disbanded without joining him, and the jealousies of the different palatinates had prevented their sending him any succours. He now begged for reinforcements to enable him to dictate peace to the Tartars, and to fortify Poland against the Turks; but the infatuated malice of the king made it difficult for him even to keep together the *December,* troops under his orders. At this juncture fatigue, and *1671.* perhaps chagrin at the treatment which he received, laid *He falls sick.* Sobieski on the bed of sickness at Zolkiew; and the king redoubled his efforts to separate him from the army. The attempt recoiled upon his own head. That body at once moved their winter quarters to the Palatinate of Russia, and formed themselves into a confederation to protect their beloved general.

But the king's attention was soon most unpleasantly diverted elsewhere. In the same month (December) an envoy from the

The Sultan declares war against Poland. Porte arrived at Warsaw, and announcing that the Cossacks had been taken under the protection of the Sublime Porte, demanded reparation for the injuries which they had suffered. No resource was left to the king's party but to treat this as a mere blind intended to conceal from Austria the Turkish advance on the side of Hungary.

The patience of the great nobles was now completely exhausted. Under the leadership of Prazmowski they entered into a con-

Confederation against the king. federation to dethrone the king. The advice of the primate was that they should take the emperor and the Polish queen into their counsels, and provide some candidate who would be ready to accept the queen's hand. Eleanor was consulted, and professed herself devoted to the plan, if they would choose Charles of Lorraine, to whom she was deeply attached. Sobieski, now convalescent, was at length made acquainted with these projects. He strongly opposed any

Joined by Sobieski. scheme which would place the country under the espionage of Austria; but being firmly convinced of the necessity of a revolution, he exhorted them to choose the brave Duke of Longueville, nephew of Condé. Prazmowski, nothing daunted, sent the queen the duke's portrait, and was assured of her acquiescence. Everything seemed favourable for the *coup d'état;* the Diet went out in a body to meet Sobieski; and the rejoicings at his recovery were universal, when suddenly news arrived that the Duke of Longueville had been slain at the passage of the Rhine (June 12th, 1672). The party of the king, and the Lithuanians, who had trembled at the coming storm, took fresh courage, while the confederates were proportionately disconcerted. Michael began to negotiate for Austrian troops to employ against the Grand General; but in the midst of the confusion it was announced that Mahomet IV. in person, with the Grand Vizier and

Invasion of the Sultan. 200,000 men, was advancing upon Kaminiec. The king's party loudly averred that this was a fabrication of their opponents; the Lithuanians swore to defend him to the death; and Sobieski, with others of the leading nobles, was proscribed. This

Sobieski proscribed. violence raised a similar storm in the Polish army in Russia, who surrounded their general, and swore to follow him to the end of the earth. "I accept your oaths," was his answer, "and the first thing I require of you is to save Poland."

Yet Poland seemed lost beyond all hope. Sobieski's troops scarcely amounted to 30,000 men, and there was now no chance

The Sultan takes Kaminiec, of uniting them to the Pospolite. The Grand General flew to Kaminiec to reinforce and provision the garrison; but he was obliged to leave it to its fate, for the governor, who belonged to the king's party, refused to admit any of his force. Kaminiec was the only great fortress which Poland possessed.

Its natural position—defended on one side by the river Smotrycz, and on the other by an inaccessible cliff—was very strong; and the Poles constantly boasted that God, who built it, would alone be able to take it. Yet so skilful were the Turkish miners, after their long experience in Candia, that it surrendered within a month.

The consternation at Warsaw was fearful. The king assembled the Pospolite at Golemba, near the capital; but his one aim was *And advances* to conclude peace on any terms. The Sultan, sending *on Leopol.* on an advanced guard to besiege Leopol, the capital of Russia, encamped at Buczacz, where amongst the Podolian mountains he enjoyed his favourite pastime of hunting. Meanwhile Sobieski had not been idle. A large body of Tartars had passed into Volhynia in support of the Turks, and, after loading themselves with spoil and with a vast train of captives, prepared to beat a retreat. Hovering always on their rear, Sobieski struck a blow whenever it was practicable, and finally caught them in a defile at Kalusz, in the Carpathian mountains. After a great carnage he dispersed them, recovered the spoil, and liberated *Victory of* nearly 30,000 Polish captives. He then formed the *Sobieski over* daring plan of a night attack on Mahomet's camp. By *the Tartars.* swift and silent marches he approached unperceived, and burst with his cavalry on the imperial tents. For a moment *His attack* the quarters of the Sultanas were in imminent danger; *upon the Sul-* but the arrival of succours put an end to the raid. *tan's camp.* With his small force Sobieski could do no more than harass the Turkish army, yet it was with indignation that he heard that the king had concluded a peace at Buczacz (October *Peace of* 18th). Michael concealed the terms as long as he could; *Buczacs.* and this increased the suspicions of the Grand General that they were dishonourable to the country. At length it was found that Podolia, the Ukraine, and Kaminiec had been ceded to the Porte, and that the king had consented to pay an annual tribute of 22,000 ducats. In return for this the Vizier withdrew his army from Polish soil; but he established a vast military camp with 80,000 men at Kotzim, on the Dniester, to overawe the vanquished nation. By this treaty, which he had no power to make without the sanction of the republic, the king of Poland reduced himself to the condition of a vassal of the Sultan.

Yet the leaders of the Pospolite at Golemba, who dreaded nothing so much as a long campaign, were loud in his defence. Suspecting *Hostility of* that Sobieski would not accept the peace, they renewed *the Pospolite* against him the sentence of proscription, and confiscated *to Sobieski.* his estates. On receiving intelligence of these attacks, Louis XIV. offered him a French dukedom and a marshal's bâton; but Sobieski would not forsake his country. Indeed his position did not justify it; for his party grew stronger day by day, while the Pospolite, ill-furnished with provisions, and rent in pieces by faction, gradually melted away. At length the queen took on herself the part of a mediator, and she was seconded by the Lithuanians, who were weary of anarchy. It then appeared how strong a hold Sobieski had upon the affections of the people. When his exploits during the war became generally known there was an immense reaction in his favour. His personal *Popularity of Sobieski.* enemies, among whom may be reckoned the king, viewed this with the utmost uneasiness, and a few of them concocted an atrocious plot against him. They suborned a poor noble, named Lodzinski, to come forward in the Diet and *Plot against him.* declare that Sobieski had sold Kaminiec to the Turks for 1,200,000 florins, and that this money had been seen in waggons on the way to its destination. This calumny raised the Diet to the highest pitch of excitement, and they would have put the slanderer in irons but for the intervention of the king. The army declared that they would wash out the insult with blood; but Sobieski calmed them, and proceeded to Warsaw to demand a trial. He was welcomed with acclamations; the palace of Wissdow, decorated with all the trophies of Zolkiewski, was placed at his disposal; and Michael sent the Grand Chamberlain to pay him his compliments. Lodzinski, when brought before a tribunal of senators and deputies, lost all courage, and confessed that he had invented *Discovered and punished.* the story for the sum of 1,000 francs—promised him by certain of the nobles. He was condemned to death; but the sentence could not be carried out without the consent of the Grand Marshal, and he was therefore suffered to live. The nobles who had been his instigators had to ask pardon on their knees.

The first object òf Sobieski in this sudden blaze of his popularity was to procure the rupture of the peace of Buczacz. He at once *He persuades the Diet not to accept the peace.* published a memorandum, setting forth necessary reforms in the administration and the army, and promising that their adoption would ensure a successful struggle against the Turks. The Diet sent him a message in high-flown Polish rhetoric, in which they begged for the presence of that hero "who, if the system of Pythagoras be true, seems to unite in his own frame the souls of all the great captains and good citizens of the past." He took his seat amid great enthusiasm (March 14th), and easily persuaded the deputies to follow his advice. They did not now dream of paying the tribute. They decreed an army of 60,000 men, the establishment of a war-tax, and the despatch of embassies for foreign aid, and finally placed in the hands of Sobieski full powers both for peace and war. This was in effect to put aside the king, and make the Grand Marshal Regent; but no voice was raised against the proposal. Since there *Their confidence in him.* was only a trifling sum remaining in the exchequer, Sobieski persuaded the Diet to use the treasure stored up as a reserve in the castle of Cracow. This, with an opportune subsidy which arrived from the Pope, was deposited with him instead of the Grand Treasurer, as the person most likely to use them to advantage.

Such unbounded confidence carried with it a responsibility which few men would have dared to face. Sobieski accepted it cheerfully, *His difficulties.* yet at the outset of the campaign he had to meet two difficulties, which he had not foreseen. His old enemy, Michael Paz, caused much delay by arriving late with his Lithuanians (Sept. 16th); and at the last moment the king announced that he should put himself at the head of the force. He came, and reviewed the troops; but during the ceremony he was seized with illness; and the next morning the Poles raised a hurra on seeing the "bonzuk," or long lance, in front of the Grand General's tent in an upright position—a sure sign that the king had quitted the army. The next day (October 11th), with a force of nearly 40,000 men, and forty small field-pieces, Sobieski began his march.

His plan of the campaign, though simple, was boldly conceived. Having heard that Caplan Pacha, with 30,000 men, was advancing *His plan of the campaign.* through Moldavia to reinforce the camp at Kotzim, he proposed to cut him off upon his march, and then to turn upon the camp itself. If he should succeed in capturing it, he hoped to isolate Kaminiec, and so to take it by blockade, and recover all that had been ceded to the Porte. He was not dismayed at the lateness of the season; for he trusted that on this account the Turks would be less willing to fight.

The banks of the Dniester were reached after three weeks' march, and here a mutiny broke out among the troops, which was *March of the army.* industriously fomented by Michael Paz. They clamoured for rest and provisions; Sobieski promised them both under the tents of the barbarians. "My resolution," said he," is not to be shaken. I intend to bury myself here or to conquer. You must do the same, or nothing can save you." His firmness had the desired effect. They crossed the Dniester and penetrated into the forest of Bucovina; but Sobieski was obliged to alter his original plans. It would have been madness to wait for Caplan Pacha and so give him time to join the camp; and yet his undisciplined soldiery shrank from the inclement plains of Moldavia. He therefore turned aside, and advanced at once on the entrenchments at Kotzim.

The castle of that name was strongly situated on the right bank of the Dniester, about twelve miles from Kaminiec. Between this *Castle and camp of Kotzim.* and the advancing Poles, at the height of twenty feet from the plain, was the vast fortified camp, unassailable on the side of the river, where the rocks were steep, and surrounded on the other sides by a broad ravine. The ground immediately in front of the entrenchments was marshy, and broken up by rapid streams, and the Turks could sweep it from end to end with their admirable artillery. Within the lines were ranged

80,000 men, the flower of the Turkish army, most of them spahis and janissaries, under the command of the Seraskier [1] Hussein.

The day after the Poles arrived (November 10th) Paz declared an assault to be impracticable, and announced his intention to *Insubordina-* retire. Sobieski replied with truth that flight was not *tion of Paz.* in their power except at the risk of extermination. The enterprise indeed seemed superhuman; but the Grand General ranged his troops in order of battle with full confidence of success. During the day a large body of Moldavians and Wallachians,[2] who occupied a spot on the left of the Turkish camp, deserted to the Poles, and greatly raised their drooping spirits. When night came on, the troops were still kept under arms, although the weather was most severe. The snow fell thickly, but Sobieski visited all the posts, and animated the men by his cheerful manner. At length he reclined on the carriage of a cannon and waited for the dawn.

It was the crisis of his great career; yet he could not but regard the scene as one of happy omen. On this spot, more than fifty *Crisis in* years before, his father had gained a splendid victory *Sobieski's life.* over the Turks, which was followed by a long peace. Then indeed the Poles were the defenders instead of the assailants of the entrenchments; but that only made the victory in prospect seem a more glorious prize.

At length the day broke, and Sobieski observed the enemy's lines much thinner than before. Many of the Turks, exhausted by the *He attacks the* unwonted cold, had sought their tents, not dreaming for *entrenchments.* one moment that the Poles would dare to attack them in daylight. "This is the moment that I waited for," cried Sobieski to his staff, and ordered at once a general assault. After galloping down the lines with a few encouraging words, he alighted from his horse, and led the infantry and his own dismounted dragoons against the entrenchments. The Turks, whose attention was distracted by a false attack on another side, left a weak point in his front, and Sobieski, though somewhat bulky, was the first to scale the parapet. He was splendidly supported by his dragoons; and the battle now raged in the midst of the tents. The infantry might possibly have been surrounded, had not Jablonowski, Palatine of Russia, dashed up a steep place with the best of the cavalry, and rushed to the rescue. Sobieski was supplied *Rout of the* with a horse, and the Turks now began to give way on *Turks,* all sides. Soliman Pacha, at the head of the janissaries, tried to retreat in good order to the plain; but he was charged by the Lithuanians in front and by the Poles in the rear,

---

[1] A "seraskier" was a commander-in-chief, who received his commission direct from the Grand Vizier.

[2] The chiefs of these principalities, now united under the name of Roumania, had been offended at the insolence of the seraskier, and their troops, being Christians, disliked serving under the Turks.

and his fine troops were cut to pieces. He is said to have himself
fallen by the hand of Sobieski, who despoiled him of his jewelled
scimitar.[1] The Turks fled in confused masses to the bridge leading
to the castle; but Sobieski had provided against this by sending
his brother-in-law, Radziwill, with a large detachment to seize it.
The only retreat now left them was the steep rock on the river-side,
from which thousands precipitated themselves into the stream; but
the Polish cavalry dashed in after them, and completed their de-
And complete struction. The carnage lasted more than three hours,
victory of the during which half the Turkish force was slain, and a
Poles. large number taken prisoners. A remnant of the original
force succeeded in escaping to Kaminiec, among whom was the
Seraskier Hussein.[2]

It is difficult to credit the statement of some historians, none of
whom are contemporaries, that Sobieski put all the prisoners to the
sword.[3] Such an act would have been opposed alike to
Question of his natural disposition and to his defensive policy.
the prisoners. Plain facts are against it; for some days later the commander at Kaminiec, delighted at the generous terms which he
granted to the garrison of the castle (November 13th,), released
fifty prisoners without ransom. Had such an enormity been com-
mitted, it must certainly have reached his ears, and would have
met with a prompt revenge.

Immediately after the victory, the Jesuit confessor of Sobieski
erected an altar in the pavilion of the Seraskier, and the whole
army, with tears of joy, attended a thanksgiving
Joy of the service. The occasion was indeed affecting, especially
Poles. to their commander. Ere long Christendom was
resounding with the praises of one who had obtained the greatest
victory over the infidel since the battle of Ascalon. Sobieski was
Their advance most anxious to follow up his success. Honour forbade
upon the him to desert the Moldavians and Wallachians, who
Danube. had come over to him at considerable risk; and he
wished to cut off from the Turks all chance of return. He put
his cavalry in motion towards the Danube with the hope of
encountering Caplan Pacha. But that general, on hearing of the
disaster at Kotzim, retreated in all haste, and took with him the
Turkish garrisons on the left bank of the Danube. Such was the
panic in Turkey that the Sultan, who had advanced to Silistria,
hurried back to his capital. But the victorious advance of the
Poles was stopped, as they were entering Wallachia, by the news
of the death of their king.

[1] *History of the Grand Viziers, Mahomet and Ashmet Cuprogli*, by F. de
Chassepol; Englished by John Evelyn, junior, published 1677. See bk. iv.
[2] Salvandy (i. 419) says Hussein was cut down by Prince Radziwill; but most
accounts agree that he escaped and died of his wounds at Kaminiec.
[3] Coyer appears to have first made this statement. It would be interesting to
know his authority. His mainstay, *Familiar Letters of the Chancellor Zaluski*, does
not support him.

On the night before the battle of Kotzim (November 10th), Michael breathed his last at Leopol. His death was caused by disease of the kidneys, but he had hastened his end by the gluttonous voracity of his appetite, which passed all bounds. He is said to have devoured in a few hours a thousand Chinese apples, presented to him by the municipality of Dantzic. His last hours were embittered by the fruits of his pusillanimous submission to the Turks. A few days before his death a Turkish Aga[1] arrived, bearing the caphtan, or robe of vassalage, which the Sultan sends to his tributaries. The king was too ill to receive him, and he had to depart without executing his commission.

Death of Michael.

The incapacity of Michael deserves our pity, because the crown was thrust upon him against his will. But he was worse than incapable. Envy and fear alternately gained the mastery over his despicable nature. His evil genius pursued him to the end. Such was the general exultation at the victory of Kotzim that there was no pretence of mourning for him; and his body was conveyed to Warsaw, almost unnoticed, beneath the triumphal arches erected in honour of his rival.

His character.

Three weeks elapsed after Michael's death before the news of the Grand General's victory arrived at Warsaw (December 4th), and in the interval the Poles had given up the army for lost. It is somewhat surprising that in a nation so excitable the sudden revulsion of feeling did not result at once in the proclamation of Sobieski. Madame de Sevigné,[2] writing just after the news arrived in Paris (December 22nd), says that there no one doubted that he would be elected. The official journals of France speak of him as "worthy of the throne which he had saved." But the Grand General himself was aware what a stormy opposition his candidature would raise among the Lithuanians. It was thus with unfeigned sorrow that he received the orders of the primate-interrex to bring back his victorious troops. Everything remained to be done towards reaping the benefits of his glorious success. The Turks were still in Kaminiec; Moldavia and Wallachia were yet to be freed; and the Cossacks who had sent in their submission had to be confirmed in their allegiance.

Exultation in Poland.

He did all he could. Though his men deserted him daily by hundreds for the more profitable field of election, he left a garrison in Kotzim, and detached 8,000 men for the defence of his two allies. Then, with a heavy heart, he retraced his steps to Leopol. He was here met by deputies from the most distant palatinates, who showered upon him their congratulations; but he showed no disposition to proceed to

Return of the Polish army.

[1] Coyer says that the Polish army, on their way to Kotzim, met this envoy.
[2] Letter 329. "La victoire du Grand Maréchal est si grand qu'on ne doute point qu'il ne soit élu roi." She does not however know much about Sobieski, for a little later (Letter 333) she represents him as of a different religion from the nation.

Warsaw. He knew too well the activity of his enemies in the Diet, and he was quite content that it should appear that he had no personal pretensions.[1]

While her late husband was still lying in state the queen had resumed her favourite project of retaining the crown by a marriage *Projects of the queen.* with Charles of Lorraine. That prince left the army of the Rhine and appeared upon the frontiers; and the emperor massed troops for his support on the borders of *Candidates.* Little Poland. Sixteen[2] other candidates appeared in the field, but many of these were Protestant princes, whose chances were small; and the contest seemed to lie between Lorraine and the young Duke of Neuberg, the son of his old antagonist. The latter, though a German prince, was supported by Louis XIV. as the heir of the Elector Palatine, and therefore *Preparations for the election.* an important ally. No artifice was spared by the queen's party to prevent the proposal of Sobieski. The Pazes brought forward a measure in the Diet for the exclusion of a Piast on account of the misfortunes of the late reign; and when this was unfavourably received, they insisted that the new king must be unmarried.[3] The Diet refused to sanction any measures of exclusion, and wrote to press for Sobieski's presence. But the hero was now at Zolkiew attending his wife in a dangerous illness, upon the origin of which various rumours were afloat. His enemies averred that he had poisoned her himself to secure the queen's hand; his friends hinted that the queen had done so to be sure of the crown at all hazards. These speculations were set at rest by the recovery of Madame Sobieska; but her husband still delayed to appear in public. He wrote, however, to the Diet, strongly urging that the threatening attitude of the Turks rendered any delay dangerous; and it was decided on this advice that the election should not be made by the whole Pospolite, but by a representative Diet. But the regulation was practically ineffective; for the Diet being held in the open air, the nobles attended as usual to watch the conduct of their deputies.

The field of Wola, close to Warsaw, was the scene of this unique spectacle. On the day when the Diet of election met *The field of election.* (April 20) all the orders of the state attended a grand service at the cathedral, and then set out on horseback for the field. In the midst of the plain was pitched the "szopa," or grand pavilion of the Senate, surrounded by a ditch to keep off intruders, and carefully closed to the public.

[1] Connor, who is evidently repeating the gossip of the king's reign, says that he "worked underhand for himself."

[2] Salvandy enumerates them (i. 430), but it can hardly be supposed that they all sent envoys. Among them were the Duke of York and his son-in-law, the Prince of Orange.

[3] Coyer says that Michael Paz, in the council of war after the battle of Kotzim, burst out with this as a condition of his supporting any candidate.

Not far off, under the open sky, sat the "kolo" or circle of deputies from the palatinates. Round it were ranged 100,000 of the nobility, jealously watching each turn of their deliberations. Every human passion found vent in this motley assemblage. Riots were frequent, and seldom ended without effusion of blood. Each noble was attended by as many valets as he could muster, who were generally a worse element of disorder than their lords. To these must be added a crowd of mercenaries from neighbouring nations, all eagerly intriguing for their national candidate. Long tables were set up as the head-quarters of each faction, and at these was heard an unceasing babel of noisy tongues. In the vacant spaces of the arena jousts were frequent, for which each palatinate brought out a splendid cavalcade. This was the occasion when all gratified the national craving for display. Many a poor noble would readily sell his vote, perhaps to more than one candidate, for the pleasure of donning a brilliant attire. Costly furs adorned their persons, and were almost hidden beneath a profusion of jewels. The same reckless display of the precious metals was seen in their accoutrements. Nor were the bishops outdone by the cavaliers. Green, broad-brimmed hats, with yellow or red pantaloons, were the common ornaments of the soldiers of the Church. Every kind of merchandise was represented. The Jews, who were ordinarily interdicted from appearing in Warsaw, made the most of the short period when the restriction was removed. The plain around the "szopa" was dotted with an immense multitude of tents, most of them devoted to buying and selling, but all decorated in the most gorgeous style. Several pavilions of superb workmanship and oriental magnificence, containing a large suite of luxurious chambers, attracted special attention. They were the quarters of the Seraskier Hussein—transported entire from the camp at Kotzim—and were now surmounted by the shield of Sobieski.

Nothing more was wanting to kindle the liveliest enthusiasm for the absent general. His name was in every mouth, and his non-appearance caused much surprise. The "kolo" *Absence of Sobieski.* elected as their marshal the Lithuanian Sapieha, a personal friend of the Grand General; and when Michael Paz pushed his hatred so far as to revive his proposal for the exclusion of a Piast (April 15), the attempt was so invidious that a party began to form in Sobieski's favour, though their designs were at first studiously concealed.

On the 2nd of May it was announced that Sobieski was approaching Warsaw. His arrival on the plain created the most *His arrival.* unbounded enthusiasm; the Diet rose and went to meet him; and his progress for miles resembled a triumph. Sixty-six banners—the spoil of Kotzim—were carried before him, to be his present, as he said, to his future king; and behind him marched a corps of captive janissaries, who were enrolled as his body-guard. Like his countrymen, he did not disdain ostentation ; for on the croup of his horse hung a shield of gold, embossed with scenes from his great career. Nature had gifted him with handsome features and a dignified mien.[1] Though stout, he was tall and erect; and his full flashing eye marked him at once as a man of frankness, bravery, and powers of observation. Yet along with his military air his face wore a sweetness of expression, which was indescribably attractive. Few of the Poles could have witnessed his entry without feeling that he was the fittest person to be their king.

Two days after (May 4) the Senate forsook the "szopa" and took their seat in the "kolo;" and Sobieski, rising in his place, *He proposes* proposed the Prince of Condé, whose military qualities, *the Prince* he said, made him the proper choice of a nation which *of Condé.* would have to struggle for its existence. This unexpected event caused an immense commotion. The vast multitude was split into the old factions of France and Austria, and for days it seemed as if there was no solution but civil war. At length (May 19) Sobieski consented to withdraw the name of Condé if the queen would consent to marry the Duke of Neuberg. Hoping against hope for the success of her party, Eleanor rejected this offer with disdain; and the Lithuanians, who were encamped on the other side of the Vistula, assumed a menacing attitude towards the Polish Pospolite. At this crisis the Bishop of Cracow, who was discharging the functions of interrex,[2] gave orders for the singing of the canticles with which the debates were accustomed to close. The familiar chant and its associations produced a dead calm in the tempestuous assembly, and at its conclusion the prelate ordered each palatinate to range itself round the banner of its *Jablonowski* palatine. While his orders were being obeyed, Jablon-*proposes* owski, palatine of Red Russia, the home of Sobieski, took *Sobieski.* advantage of the silence to address all those within hearing. He represented Lorraine as too devoted to the empire, Neuberg as too young, Condé as too old, to command their armies with vigour. The times, he said, required a prince who was well acquainted alike with them and with their military system. He was here interrupted with loud shouts of "A Piast!" a sound which soon collected round the speaker all the surging masses of the Pospolite. The palatine continued, "Among ourselves is a man whose sacrifices for his country have caused him to be everywhere considered the first of the sons of Poland. In placing him at our head we shall do no more than consecrate his own glory; fortunate

[1] Dr. South describes him as follows : "He is a tall, corpulent prince, large-faced, and full eyes, and goes always in the same dress with his subjects, with his hair cut round about his ears like a Monk, and wears a fur cap, extraordinarily rich with diamonds and jewels, large whiskers, and no neck-cloth."—*Letter to Dr. Pococke,* p. 5.
[2] Czartoryski, Archbishop of Guesna, had died suddenly at a banquet given by Sobieski.

to be able to honour by one title the more the remainder of a life, of which every day has been dedicated to the republic. We know that such a king will maintain our nation in the rank which it occupies in the world. Such a man as he is will never make himself a vassal of the infidel. Poles, if we are deliberating here in peace on the election of a king, if the most illustrious dynasties are courting our suffrages, if our liberty remains secure, if even we have a country left to us, to whom do we owe it? Remember the marvels of Slobodyszcza, of Podhaic, of Kalusz, above all, of Kotzim, and take for your king John Sobieski!"[1]

A tempest of applause followed this speech, and as it subsided the voice of one of the castellans was heard calling upon the Poles to elect that man whom the Turks would be most anxious to exclude. Then from the midst of the host rose loud shouts of "Long live King John Sobieski!" and thirteen palatinates at once took up the cry. The regular soldiers pressed forward towards the szopa, exclaiming, "We will all perish together, or have for our king John Sobieski!" It was already late in the evening, but the Polish nobility crowded round the interrex, and besought him to take the votes. One voice alone was raised against the proposition;

He postpones the voting. it was that of Sobieski. He firmly declared that he could not accept the crown if it was offered at the fall of night, and in a manner so sudden that no one could have time to recollect himself. "If," said he, "there is no other protest against the election being made this night, I shall oppose my veto." This disinterested advice was unwillingly followed, and Sobieski left the plain to encounter the reproaches of his wife.

Several writers—principally the later Polish historians, who treat him with marked disfavour—endeavour to detect in his conduct *And shows his fair dealing.* throughout the proceedings the signs of crafty intrigue. Yet by this last step he allowed his enemies time to combine against him, and gave the queen's party a fair opportunity of reviving their scattered energies. But such generosity is often the best policy. The succeeding night and day (May 20th) were spent in a general effort to secure unanimity; and the riches and influence of his brother-in-law, Radziwill, were of much service to Sobieski in the Lithuanian camp. But his own popularity was still more effectual. It had ever been the privilege of the Grand General of Poland to quarter his army where he pleased, and pay nothing for their maintenance. Bribes had formerly been freely taken from those districts that desired exemption,[2] but Sobieski, unwilling to exercise such tyranny, had always

---

[1] Three contemporary authorities give this eloquent speech *in extenso;* and the language which is common to all of them, and which is here quoted, enables us to understand its electrical effect upon the audience.

[2] This generally occurred on Church lands, for nobles could make themselves heard against the general in the Diet. Daleyrac (chap. i. p. 12) says that he had heard of these officers making 6,000 francs by bribes.

quartered his army on the frontiers. This was now remembered
with gratitude. His promises to the republic also

His offers to
the republic. became the topic of admiring conversation. He engaged
to pay the pension to the queen dowager, to redeem the
crown jewels, to found a military school for the young nobility, to
build two fortresses wherever the Diet should appoint, and to
furnish the regular army with six months' pay. Early in the day
two of the family of Paz came to register their opposition with
the interrex, but before night fell they had been persuaded to

Proclamation
of Sobieski. forego it. The next morning Sobieski was proclaimed
king amid the acclamations of both Principalities, and
took the name of John III. The same day a vast
crowd attended him to the cathedral of St. John to return thanks
for his election.

Europe in general was less astonished at his elevation than
Poland. At Constantinople and at Vienna alone the news was

Opinion of
Europe. received with disfavour. Köprili saw less chance of
recovering his conquests; and the emperor was bitterly
mortified to see upon the throne one who had always
belonged to the faction of France. Poland was daily becoming of
greater importance in the struggle between Louis and Leopold.
When the republic was bleeding from the shocks of her barbarous
neighbours, and from a succession of internal troubles, it mattered
little to these great potentates who filled the throne; but now that
she had proved herself strong enough to withstand the dreaded
Turk, and wise enough to offer the crown to her victorious general,
she was looked upon with a respect to which she had hitherto
been a stranger. This was fully appreciated at the Papal Court.
Clement X., besides his benediction, sent assurances of friendship
to the new king; and Oliva, the general of the Jesuits, wrote his
joyful congratulations to "the pillar of the republic and the
avenger of Christendom." It is difficult to discover how far the
court of France had a hand in his election. Its ambassador,
Forbin-Janson, bishop of Marseilles, arrived somewhat late (May
8th), and certainly brought instructions to support the Duke of
Neuberg. But he probably discovered ere long which way the
tide was setting, and, adapting himself to circumstances with a
Frenchman's ready wit, he caused it to be supposed that he had
used his influence in favour of Sobieski. Louis XIV. followed
the same course; and in an official note of the same summer
claimed this election as one more instance of the universal triumph
of his policy.

The machinations of the enemies of Sobieski did not cease with
the withdrawal of their veto. Their first move was to give notice

Schemes of
the king's
enemies. of a law which should oblige him to divorce his wife
and marry the queen dowager. But on this point the
king was firm. " I have not yet finally promised," said
he, "to accept the royal functions. If this is the price of your

sceptre, you need not offer it." The proposal was soon dropped; and Eleanor, after receiving a visit from the king, retired to Thorn, whence she still exercised a baneful influence upon the course of affairs. Four years later (1678) she gave her hand to her old suitor, the Prince of Lorraine.

Whilst the Diet was drawing up the *pacta conventa*, Sobieski discovered from an examination of his revenues that he could not fulfil his promise of paying the army for six months. Without delay he frankly owned his inability; and his opponents made this a pretext for inserting in the contract new restrictions on the military authority of the king. They also wished to bind him to an eternal alliance with the court of Vienna. It was soon known that the king would not yield to these terms; and several stormy scenes took place in the Diet. At length the obnoxious articles were struck out; and on the 5th June the king received the instrument of his election from the hands of the interrex.

There now remained only the ceremony of coronation—which was a necessary prelude to the exercise of the royal functions.

Danger from the Turks. But the steady advance of the Turks grew daily more disquieting. Caplan Pacha had rallied the remnants of the defeated force, and the Sultan was already marching with a great army through Bulgaria. John saw that the delay would be dangerous, and had the courage to disappoint the queen' and the whole court by deferring the ceremony. He told the Senate that at such a time a helmet became his forehead better than a diadem. "I know well," said he, "that I have been elected, not to represent the republic, but to fight for her. I will first fulfil my mission." Touched by his magnanimity, the Diet resolved to place in his hands at once all the powers of a king.

Meantime the Turks, accompanied by the Tartars, had appeared in great force before the camp at Kotzim. The Polish commander, terrified at their numbers, soon surrendered, and the *They invade the Ukraine.* whole garrison was put to the sword. But instead of advancing into the heart of Poland, Köprili turned to the right into the Ukraine, where the Muscovites, who also laid claim to that territory, now lined the Borysthenes with 100,000 men. Hearing that he was occupied in besieging small places in the Ukraine, John promised to render a good account of him before the close of the campaign. He kept his word. While the Turks drove the Muscovites beyond the river, he suddenly appeared in *Campaign of 1674.* Podolia and besieged Bar. The Sultan, who was distracted by news of intrigues at his capital and the advance of the Sophy upon Babylon, suddenly broke up his camp, and made for Silistria. The Tartars disappeared at the sound of "the Polish hurricane," as they called Sobieski; and John

---

[1] No queen of Poland was entitled to any allowance from the republic (or pension in case of widowhood) without having been crowned.

was left to deal with the hapless country which had but just suffered from the Ottoman invasion. He could see no mode of protecting its peasants from the yoke of the nobility but to place his *John winters* army in winter quarters in the neighbourhood, and to *in the* teach the cavalry by his own example what clemency *Ukraine.* and what self-sacrifice they ought to show towards a subject people. Resistance was only to be expected; for his haughty hussars had never before passed a winter away from their estates. But when they saw their king take up his abode in the miserable town of Braclaw, where the scarcity of forage increased the hardships of the season, the Polish cavalry submitted without a murmur.

Not so, however, did the Lithuanians. The king had assigned to Paz the town of Bar, the most comfortable post on the frontiers. *The Lithu-* Yet that general did not approve of the innovation, and *anians desert* taking the law into his own hands marched home with *him.* his army. This defection was a great blow to the king. He had begun to invest Kaminiec, and had opened negotiations for an alliance with Muscovy. He now saw himself obliged to narrow his plans, and to confine himself to the defensive. The desertion of Paz aroused the strongest indignation in Poland, and he was forced to ask the king's pardon; but he could not now repair the mischief. His disbanded troops were amusing themselves with pillaging their own country,[1] and there was no chance at present of rallying them round their standards.

The winter passed without any important success; and early in April another large Turkish army, commanded by Ibrahim Pacha,[2] nicknamed "Schischman" from his enormous bulk, *Campaign* advanced into Volhynia. John hastily quitted the *of 1675.* Ukraine and disposed his small forces for the defence of Russia in a vast arc, of which Leopol was the centre. So completely was he outnumbered that his only chance of success seemed to lie in procuring allies. He continued to treat with the Czar, and received at Leopol with ostentatious pomp an ambassador from the Sophy of Persia; but he could hope little from the latter, except the chance of terrifying the Sultan by a supposed coalition with his Asiatic enemy.

Meanwhile Ibrahim had copied the fault of the preceding year by wasting time in small sieges, and it was not till he received a threatening message from Köprili that he began to *Lethargy of* advance upon the Polish force covering Leopol, which *the Poles.* hardly amounted to 15,000 men. No exertions on the part of the king could awaken Poland to a sense of its danger.

[1] Daleyrac (ch. i. p. 11) says that the Lithuanians are a worse scourge to the country than the Tartars. We shall find them as barbarous to the friendly people of Hungary.

[2] Coyer makes the astounding mistake of stating that Köprili died in 1674, and was succeeded in the command in Poland by Kara Mustapha. (pp. 210, 216, 8vo ed.)

Servitude had numbed the senses of the peasants, and the nobles were wearied with the length of the war. Ibrahim seemed unwilling to trust his fortune against that of Sobieski. Sitting down before Trembowla, a strong fortress in Podolia, he sent on the Tartar Noureddin with 40,000 men "to bring the king before him dead or alive."

It was late in August when this detachment [1]—the flower of the Turkish army—arrived at Leopol, and began to burn the suburbs.

Battle of Leopol. The Poles besought the king to retire, and not risk his life in so deadly a combat. "You would despise me," said he, "if I were to follow your advice." The ground in the vicinity was undulating and covered with vineyards, and John carefully made his dispositions in order to conceal from the enemy the smallness of his force. He planted several hills, which he could not occupy, with the spare lances of his hussars, and concealed squadrons in the valleys near the point of attack. Then, on the 24th of August, amidst a storm of snow and hail which beat in the faces of the enemy, he suddenly charged the infidels at the head of 5,000 cavalry, repeating thrice the name of Jesus. The impetuous bravery of the Poles spread terror in the Turkish ranks, and before nightfall the whole force, though at least eight times the number of their assailants, had fled in disorder. The storm was so unusual for the time of year that contemporary memoirs speak of it as miraculous; and it appears that this battle, more than any other, contributed to cause the superstitious fear with which the Turkish troops subsequently regarded John Sobieski.

Ibrahim was dismayed at the king's success. He had captured the position of Podhaic, but he could not reduce the garrison of

Siege of Trembowla. Trembowla, commanded by Chrasonowski, a man of determined courage. He now redoubled his assault upon that place, which must have fallen but for the arrival of John with the Polish army. The king posted his troops to advantage and prepared for the attack; but during the night (Oct. 6th) Ibrahim intercepted a letter to the besieged, which informed him that the king in person was at the head of the Poles. He at once raised the siege, and without striking a blow retreated precipitately

Retreat of the Turks. to Kaminiec, and thence across the Danube. John would have pursued him beyond the outskirts of Podolia, but the Polish vanguard, dreading a winter's campaign in the enemy's country, set fire to the bridges, and compelled their king to suspend his march.

The whole country clamoured for his return, and the Diet was impatient to return thanks to its deliverer. The Vice-chancellor declared in the Senate that the king moved like a tortoise towards the throne, but like an eagle towards the enemies of the

---

[1] The account followed by Salvandy (ii. 29) represents the whole Turkish army, nearly 200,000 strong, as having been present. Coyer, following Zaluski, gives the account in the text.

republic.   He was now ready to gratify the general wish, and
returning to Zolkiew received a number of foreign am-
Return of
the king.   bassadors sent to congratulate him upon his election,—
among them Lawrence Hyde, Earl of Rochester,[1] whom
Dr. South was attending as domestic chaplain.   The French ambassador solicited John's alliance against Brandenburg and the
empire, and held out hopes of persuading the Turks to make
peace.   But the king deferred all fresh engagements for the
present; his grand aim in life was to save Poland from the
Ottoman grasp.

Cracow was, as usual, the scene of the coronation, which was
fixed for the 2nd of February (1676).   Two days earlier, according
Burial of the   to the Polish custom, John followed to the grave the
two last kings.   body of Michael, and the interest of the ceremony was
deepened on this occasion by the obsequies of Casimir.
The ex-king had died three years before, of grief, it was said, at the
fall of Kaminiec.[2]   The reigns of the two deceased kings, so fruit-
ful in misfortunes to Poland, comprised the whole of Sobieski's
wonderful career, and it was fitting that their royal mourner should
be he to whose prowess they were chiefly indebted for retaining the
Coronation.   crown.   The coronation took place amid general rejoicings, broken only by a few murmurs when the crown
was set upon the queen's head.   It was not long before she showed
her unfitness to wear it.

Two days later (February 4th) the Diet met, and was conspicuous
for its loyal enthusiasm.   The king was entreated not to lay down
Diet of 1676.   the office of Grand General, but he wisely refused a
privilege so invidious, and conferred the post upon his
old enemy, Demetrius Wiesnowiescki.   He displayed the same
generous spirit in his other appointments, offering the primacy to
Olzowski, the favourite of Eleanor, and the Grand Marshalate to
Lubomirski, son of his old rival.   The brave Jablonowski was
rewarded with the post of Second General.   His elevation caused
some trouble.   The Diet proposed to make these dignities
triennial, which, in the present reign at least, would have been a
salutary enhancement of the royal power; but the queen, out of
gratitude to Jablonowski, worked hard in secret to defeat the proposal.   The king, though he favoured it at heart, appeared neutral;
and the project fell through.

John availed himself of the favourable temper of the Diet to
take exceptional measures for the national defence.   He proposed
a capitation subsidy upon all alike, clergy as well as laity, and
strongly urged the necessity of forming a permanent infantry.
Hitherto this branch of the service had been fixed at one-third of
the regular army (16,000), but it had never reached this standard,

---

[1] He had been previously received by John in the camp at Leopol.   The German
name for that town is Lemberg.
[2] He died of apoplexy on receiving the intelligence.

and being composed only of the peasants and poorer nobles, commanded by foreign officers, its equipment was disgracefully inefficient.[1] The Diet voted that the army should be raised to 73,000 men, thus augmenting it by 25,000,[2] and that of these 35,000 should be infantry. No king had ever obtained such concessions from the nobility, but they were not granted without a violent opposition. The old expedient was tried of drawing out the Diet, but John defeated it by submitting to a continuous sitting, and presiding upon the throne for forty consecutive hours. He was able to announce that the Great Elector had promised him succours, and that he hoped for an alliance with Muscovy. The Diet did not rise before paying him the unusual compliment of a decree that all the starosties which he had held should remain hereditary in his family.[3]

Unfortunately their good resolutions were not carried into effect. Although the Dietines ratified their proceedings, it was beyond the king's power to overcome the inertness and lethargy of *The king fails to levy troops.* the nobility. The patriotic spirit died out at once when the magic of his personal influence was withdrawn. Seizing upon a rumour which was industriously raised by Austria, that the king was treating in secret with the Turks and would use the money for his own purposes, they refused to pay the subsidy, and threw every obstacle in his way. John hastily assembled at Leopol those troops which had not been disbanded; but, although their number is variously stated, some even placing it as low as 10,000, it probably did not amount to one-half of the force that the Diet had decreed.

Meanwhile, Köprili had not been idle. He assembled an army of 100,000 Turks, to be accompanied by a vast host of Tartars. *Armament of the Turks.* But his aim was more pacific than in the former campaigns. He was beset by the proffered mediation of the European powers, especially of Louis XIV., who wished to evade his promise of sending armed assistance to Poland. Moreover, the condition of Asiatic Turkey distracted his attention; his allies, the Cossacks and the Tartars, inspired him with distrust; and he felt that his fortune was outshone by the star of John Sobieski. The name of the Polish hero was such a terror in the Ottoman ranks that threats alone could induce many of the officers to serve against him. Köprili looked out anxiously for a competent general. He chose Ibrahim, Pacha of Damascus, called "Shaitan" (Satan), from his combined bravery and cunning, and gave him instructions to procure an honourable peace.

[1] Daleyrac (ch. i. 22). The infantry formed the rear guard, and when composed of Cossacks, were useful in a dangerous retreat.

[2] The regular army, called "Komport," or sometimes "Quartians," was supposed to consist of 48,000 men, of which 12,000 were Lithuanians; but it hardly ever reached this amount. (Daleyrac, ch. i.)

[3] This was a most valuable addition to his revenue.

Ibrahim secretly hoped to do more than this, for he was confident that he could drive the king to extremities. He pushed on at once into Galicia and crossed the Dniester, expecting that John would attack him; but finding that the king lay inactive at Zurawno, a small town on the left bank, he advanced against him without delay. John called in his squadrons of horse, which had been harassing the Tartars, and prepared to improve his position. It had been chosen with admirable judgment. He lay with the Dniester and the mountains behind it covering his rear, while his left rested on the town of Zurawno, and his right was protected by woods and marshes. In front of his lines ran a rapid torrent, called the Swiczza, which was easily fordable, and offered facilities for the construction of entrenchments. On this task John employed his whole army, and collected all the provisions within reach. When the seraskier appeared on the heights in his front, he left his lines and offered him battle (September 25th); but this was declined, for all the Turkish troops had not yet come up. Ibrahim, when he had assembled them, formed them into a vast arc, including the town of Zurawno, the Polish army, and the wood on its right, with each of his wings resting on the river. He then commenced a regular siege. His artillery was splendidly handled; and his miners rapidly approached the Polish entrenchments. John at once employed counter-mines, but the experience of the Turks in Candia gave them a vast superiority. The king was anxious to bring on a general action, and in a skirmish on the 29th of September the Poles had the advantage, but they lost heavily. John's situation was becoming desperate; the Tartars who commanded the river prevented the arrival of provisions by that route; and the Turkish artillery made frightful havoc in his ranks.

Invasion of Galicia.

Siege of Zurawno.

The liveliest alarm prevailed in Poland. The Senate called out the Pospolite and placed Prince Radziwill at its head; but the assembling of such a body was necessarily slow. Meantime another engagement took place at Zurawno (October 8th), in which 2,000 Turks were slain; but John failed to break through the enemy's lines, and was once nearly surrounded and cut off from his men by a body of janissaries. When however the siege had lasted nearly twenty days, the Tartar khan, whose dominion was menaced by the Muscovites,[1] pressed Ibrahim to conclude a peace. The Seraskier knew the straits to which the Poles were reduced, and he therefore sent an envoy to propose the ratification of the treaty of Buczacz and an offensive alliance against Muscovy. John replied shortly that he would hang the next man who brought him such a message.

Proposals of peace.

---

[1] Coyer says that the Muscovites were advancing into Poland to the king's relief, but this seems improbable.

The bombardment recommenced, and the soldiers murmured against their king's obstinacy. Paz repaired to the royal tent and announced his intention to desert. "Desert who will," cried John, "the Turks shall not reach the heart of the republic without passing over my corpse." He then rode down the ranks, and reminding the soldiers that he had extricated them from many a worse plight, he gaily asked them if his head were enfeebled by the weight of a crown. Yet he passed the night in the gravest anxiety, and when morning broke (October 14th) he quitted his lines and drew up his whole force in order of battle.

Refused by the king.

The Turks were astounded; and the Tartars cried out that there was magic in his boldness. Brave though he was, Ibrahim dared not face the chances of a defeat. He knew that the Pospolite was approaching; he suspected that the Tartars had been bought over; and he saw winter rapidly closing in. Above all, he remembered that his instructions were pacific, and that a serious reverse might cost him his head.

Ibrahim proposes fairer terms.

Before the armies engaged, he proposed a peace upon honourable terms. No mention was now made of tribute. The Porte was to retain only Kaminiec and a third of the Ukraine; the question of Podolia was referred to a subsequent conference; each army was to restore its prisoners of war. It is said that Sobieski, with the sentiments of a Christian knight, inserted an article to provide for the establishment of a Latin guard at the Holy Sepulchre.[1] After witnessing the release of 15,000 captives, and the departure of the Turks (October 16th), John retraced his steps to Zolkiew. He soon encountered the Pospolite, which was advancing to his relief, and the two armies celebrated the conclusion of peace with a grand flourish of trumpets.

Peace of Zurawno.

Though satisfactory, the terms were not glorious; but that they should have been obtained at all by a handful of men in the direst extremities was cause enough for rejoicing. A moral triumph like this, following so close upon a crisis so dreadful, carries with it an air of romance. Yet, making every allowance for good fortune and the earnest mediation of his allies, we must regard it as due in the first instance to the potency of the name of Sobieski. With an insignificant force at his back he had conducted to a favourable issue five successive campaigns against the Turks—four of them on Polish ground—and had previously many times repulsed the hordes of Tartars which they had poured into the country. By thus foiling the aggression of the Turks when at the height of their power John III. had rendered a signal service to Europe.

Great services of the king.

[1] Coyer implies that the condition was refused, Ibrahim scornfully remarking that the Greeks, who then held the holy places, were Christians as well as the Latins.

The minister whose vast designs he had thwarted was now upon his death-bed. Seven days after the peace of Zurawno (October 23rd), Köprili expired at Constantinople. Had it not been for Sobieski this able vizier would have extended the dependencies of Turkey from the Black Sea to the Baltic, and would have found a golden opportunity for his attack upon the empire. His successor Mustapha, called "Kara," or "the Black," was a man of a different calibre. He owed his advancement to the intrigues of the seraglio; he had married a daughter of the Sultan and possessed great influence over his master; and he inherited the ambitious dreams of Köprili without his ability to realise them.

Death of Köprili.

All Europe, with the exception perhaps of Austria, rejoiced at the peace of Zurawno. Madame de Sevigné, writing on the 18th of November, 1676, expresses the general admiration for the hero of Poland;[1] and Condé sent a special messenger to congratulate his friend. Louis XIV. eagerly sought his alliance. He commissioned his ambassador in Poland, the Marquis of Bethune, brother-in-law of the king, to invest him with the order of the Holy Ghost. John imprudently accepted the honour, and thus, in spite of the enthusiasm with which he had been received, excited general murmurs. He was accused of wearing the livery of France, and binding the republic to follow her interests. In the Diet which assembled the next year (January, 1677,) his opponents were clamorous. They complained that, besides part of the Ukraine, he had given up Kaminiec, the key of the realm; and that instead of striving to recover them, he was meditating war against Brandenburg and Austria. They also accused him of aiming at absolute power by the secret help of the French monarch. The majority of the Diet, however, did not forget the dangers from which they had been rescued; and Gninski, palatine of Kulm, was sent to Constantinople to ratify the peace of Zurawno.

Enthusiasm of Europe.

No notice was taken of the other charges; yet John was undoubtedly conniving at the designs of France. Louis XIV. had promised assistance to the insurgents in Hungary against the emperor, and was encouraging Sweden to attack the Great Elector. It is said that he gained over Sobieski by the promise of ducal Prussia and a larger frontier on the Baltic. At any rate the Marquis of Bethune was allowed to raise troops destined for Hungary in the starosties of the king, while secret permission was given to the Swedes to pass through Courland to attack the Elector.[2] Frederic William naturally

He supports the designs of France.

---

[1] Letter 537. "La paix de Pologne est faite, mais romanesquement. Ce héros, à la tête de quinze mille hommes, entourés de deux cent mille, les a forcés, l'épée à la main, à signer la traité. Il s'était campé si avantageusement que depuis La Calprenède on n'avait rien vu de pareil."

[2] The expedition was made and failed ignominiously.

resented the attitude of Poland, and in revenge fomented some disturbances which had arisen in Dantzic.

This prosperous centre of commerce enjoyed, as a Hanse town, a large share of independence. Though belonging to the republic of Poland, it was governed by its own magistrates and *Disturbances in Dantzic,* its own laws. A religious struggle had broken out between the magistrates, who were Calvinists, and the people, who were headed by an eloquent Lutheran preacher. John at once visited the city and mediated between the contending parties (September, 1677), and the unusual spectacle was presented of a Catholic acting as arbiter in a Protestant dispute. *Quieted by the king.* His moderation won all hearts, and tranquillity was soon restored. The astronomer Hevelius, who was one of the chief citizens, entertained the king in his house, and entitled his newly-found constellation, "Scutum Sobieski."[1]

John was recalled from Dantzic by the serious intelligence that the new Grand Vizier was placing every obstacle in the way of the conclusion of peace. He kept the Polish envoy for *Activity of the Turks.* months at the gates of Constantinople; and when at length he gave him an audience, his tone was haughty and unconciliatory. The Austrian court, fearing for itself, had done its utmost to persuade the Porte that the peace of Zurawno was disgraceful to Turkey, and Mustapha, who longed for military glory, encouraged the idea. His first blow, however, was to fall on Muscovy. The Czar Feodor hastened to conclude the treaty with Poland, which had long been pending, but he could look for no assistance from the republic. He was worsted in the campaign which followed, but the vizier, disgusted at the rigour of the climate, looked out for a more alluring prey. His first thought was to reopen the war with Poland; and he announced that he should keep her envoy as a hostage until Podolia was ceded to the Porte (September, 1678).

John now saw clearly that the danger from Turkey was still pressing. He therefore at once withdrew his support from the *Coldness of John towards France.* French designs in the west, and prepared to confront his old enemy. This change in his policy is reasonable enough. He saw that the Hungarian insurgents would *Reasons.* probably call in the Porte, and in that case his natural ally would be Austria, while from France he could expect no material help. His judgment was most sagacious; but it was not uninfluenced by personal reasons. He was offended at the pride of the French king, who had refused him on his accession the coveted title of "Majesty," and had lately treated his queen with some contempt. Immediately after her coronation, his queen had set out for France to take the waters of Bourbon,[2] and to display

[1] Palmer, *Memoirs of Sobieski.* See also *Biographie Universelle,* art. "Hevelius."
[2] Bourbon l'Archambault, in the department of Allier.

her dignity in her native country; but on her way she encountered the French ambassador, who delicately hinted that his master could not receive an elective queen with full honours. The " Grand Monarque " could not stoop to receive on equal terms the daughter of the captain of his brother's Swiss Guards. The queen retraced her steps in great indignation, which subsequent events only tended to increase. Through her husband she begged a dukedom for her father, the Marquis d'Arquien, but Louis, though his language was fair, deferred compliance.[1] Moreover, John could not but regard with disgust the scarcely concealed efforts of France to set the Turks in motion against the house of Austria. The king himself had throughout his life distrusted Austria and counteracted her influence in Poland, but his chivalrous spirit would have revolted from bringing the infidel against her. He now perceived that it was his policy to make common cause with her.

He was anxious to strike the first blow against the Turks by surprising Kaminiec, which was poorly guarded; but for this the consent of the Diet was necessary. He had to publish *His designs upon Kaminiec.* his universals[2] to the Dietines describing his projects, and to debate the question in the Diet when assembled. This year (1679) it was convened at Grodno, in Lithuania, and so stormy was the session that it was four months before the king's proposal passed. The Turks were thus enabled to strengthen and re-victual the town at their leisure; and nothing was left to the king but to send ambassadors to the European courts to propose a general league against the Sultan.

A vast armament was in preparation at Constantinople, and no one in Europe knew against whom it would first be directed. *Arming of the Turks.* Troops were daily arriving from the interior of Asia, and Greece was made subject to a searching levy. It was plainly time for the European powers to show themselves united against the common enemy, but there was little prospect of such a combination. Louis had lately concluded a peace with the Emperor at Nimeguen (1679), but it was scarcely more than a suspension of hostilities.

The Polish ambassador, Radziwill, had no success at the court of Vienna. He could not persuade Leopold that he was in greater *Polish Embassies in Europe.* danger than Poland. But his proposals were not merely defensive. He urged the formation of a league, " which should hurl back the monster into his native deserts, and revive from its ruins the ancient empire of Byzantium."[3] But when he arrived at Rome (July, 1680) he found

---

[1] He alleged as his reason the poverty of the marquis. Some scandal was caused by the attempt of the French queen to secure this honour for a certain Brisacier, her attendant, who represented himself as the natural son of Sobieski during his visit to France. John could not remember the circumstances, and the French queen afterwards denied that she wrote to him upon the subject. The affair was never explained.

[2] In which he summoned the Diet and enumerated the agenda.

[3] Oratio principis Radziwill ad Imperatorem.

the Pope very favourably disposed towards a crusade. The chair was now filled by Innocent XI., an Austrian by birth, who feared that Vienna was the object of attack, and saw at once that Italy must stand or fall with it. He had been formerly Papal Nuncio in Poland, and in that capacity had bestowed his blessing on the marriage of Sobieski. He now promised his hearty aid to the king, whom he styled, "The invincible lieutenant of the God of armies, that brazen wall against which all the efforts of the barbarians have been dashed in pieces." He agreed forthwith to furnish a large subsidy.

This close alliance with the Pope widened the breach between Sobieski and the court of France. There could be no peace between such haughty characters as Innocent XI. and *Alliance with the Pope.* Louis XIV., and they were often at open enmity about the Gallican clergy. Louis hated the Pope above all things for his sympathy with the Austrian court. He now sought to counteract his influence by sending as ambassador to Warsaw Forbin-Janson, at this time bishop of Beauvais, who was to be assisted by Vitry, a man of great resource.

When the king assembled the next Diet at Warsaw (Jan. 1681) he found the French party for the first time arrayed against him. He had to report that his embassies had met with com- *Diet of 1681.* plete success only at Rome, but that Savoy and Portugal had sent him their good wishes. The majority of the Diet supported him in his schemes against the Porte; but French intrigue protracted the session for months, and finally dissolved it by the veto on a frivolous pretext. Indignant at these proceedings, Innocent XI., during his lifetime, withheld from Forbin-Janson the Cardinal's hat, which had been promised him at the accession of Sobieski. Fortunately, however, the Grand Vizier suddenly assumed a peaceful attitude towards Poland, and sent an envoy *Peace with Turkey.* with conditions which she could honourably accept. Mustapha was evidently bent on some more vast design; but though he studiously concealed its nature, John seems to have divined it from the first.

He spent the two succeeding years in strengthening and disciplining his army, and in those peaceful employments to which he was so much attached. At a wild spot, six miles from *1681-2.* Warsaw, he constructed his palace of Willanow, and introduced on his estate the Dutch system of farming. For a time all the clamours of faction were hushed; but it was only the calm which heralds the approaching storm.

Louis XIV. had never abandoned his encroachments upon the empire. At the end of 1681 he availed himself of a legal fiction, created by his own "Chambers of Reunion," to occupy *Designs of Louis XIV.* Strasburg, Casale, and other important towns on the imperial frontier. The Diet of Ratisbon vehemently protested against this spoliation, but in vain. They did not dare to provoke him to open war; for it was known that his envoys were strongly urging the Turks to invade Austria. His plan seems to have been to acquire the glory of saving the Empire after the fall of its capital, and to exact in return for his services large territorial concessions. His ambition was to have the Dauphin proclaimed king of the Romans.

At length his policy seemed on the point of success. Kara *The Turks* Mustapha threw off the mask (1682), and declaring *protect Hun-* Hungary tributary to the Sultan, announced his inten- *gary.* tion of protecting the new province. Count Emeric Tekeli, who had ably headed its revolt since 1678, was invested with the caphtan as hospodar. Leopold vainly endeavoured, by his minister Caprara, to obtain a renewal of the peace made *Schemes of* with the Turks in 1664; but the influence of France in *Leopold.* the divan was too strong for him. He then turned to the Diet at Ratisbon;[1] but its counsels were divided, the western electors being in favour of war with France. His only hope seemed to be an alliance with Poland, yet his relations with the king were not cordial, and he had lately refused his offer of a league. He made the attempt, however, and succeeded beyond his hopes. John was convinced that the peace which he had concluded with the Turks was merely temporary. It therefore seemed his duty to strike at once while he could be sure of an ally. Such a course was in keeping with his life-long purpose to curb the Ottoman power. It also agreed well with the hatred which his queen had conceived against the court of France, and the promise of an archduchess for his son was not to be despised.

Louis left no stone unturned to divert him from his resolution. He tempted him with the provinces of Silesia and Hungary, to *Offers of* become the property not of the republic but of the king *France to* and his heirs, if he would join him against the Empire; *the king.* and finding him proof against his offers he began a *French* conspiracy to dethrone him. On the assembling of the *conspiracy* next Diet (January 27th, 1683) the heat of parties was *against him.* tremendous. When Leopold's ambassador, the Count of Walstein, and Palaviccini, the Papal Nuncio, had stated their proposals of alliance, the deputies in the pay of France put in their protest. Besides placing every obstacle in the way of public business, they appealed to the outside public. Pamphlets appeared daily in which the policy of the king was warmly condemned. The selfish cabinet of Austria, which had refused to save Poland, was declared her eternal enemy, and the nobles were warned that the king could not ally himself with such a court without imbibing its despotic views.

The opposition gathered strength, and the consequences might

[1] The Diet afterwards sent succours to the relief of Vienna, and the electors of Bavaria and Saxony each commanded a contingent.

have been serious had not the king fortunately intercepted some letters of the French ambassador, which disclosed the details of his plot (March). He read these letters in full Diet, and their contents excited the utmost indignation. The ambassador boasted that through Morstyn, the Grand Treasurer, he knew all the secrets of the cabinet, that he had bought over numbers of the principal nobles, whose names he gave, and that the nation was so venal that he felt certain of destroying the league. He added that the king had rejected all his offers, but that he trusted to make him powerless. Among the nobles mentioned were Jablonowski, now Grand General of Poland, and Sapieha, who, since the death of Michael Paz, had been Grand General of Lithuania. The latter belonged to a family upon which the king had showered his favours.

Discovered by the king.

John used this information with wonderful tact. He at once declared that the ambassador, to show his zeal to his master, had evidently slandered the grandees; Morstyn alone, whose guilt was proved by a letter in his own hand, deserved the punishment of treason. The king concluded by saying that he trusted the Diet would help him to show the French king that the Polish nation was not altogether venal. The speech was received with shouts of applause, and the suspected nobles were now foremost in supporting the king. A similar change took place in the nation, and the French ambassador found it unsafe to go abroad without an escort. The Grand Treasurer would have been brought to trial if he had not escaped to France.

His tact.

The immediate result of this discovery was the conclusion of an alliance, offensive and defensive, with Austria (March 31st). Leopold bound himself to bring 60,000 men into the field; the republic was to furnish 40,000. There was an express stipulation that neither party should apply to the Pope for leave to break his oaths. The Papal Nuncio procured the addition of a clause, by which John bound himself to command his troops in person.[1] Leopold in return conceded to him that title of "Majesty" which he had so long withheld.

Alliance with the empire.

This treaty was a serious blow to the policy of Louis XIV. Forbin-Janson, who soon quitted Poland in disgust, comforted his master by the assurance that John was far too unwieldy to take the field. The same idea prevailed throughout Europe, and especially in the Turkish camp. He was now so stout that he required aid to mount his horse; but he had not lost one spark of his youthful fire. His army needed complete reorganisation, and he spent several hours each day in the field. He did not neglect measures of policy. He proposed to the Emperor the extension of the league, and confided to him his favourite scheme of reviving a republic in Greece. By that means

Exertions of Sobieski.

---

[1] DALEYRAC, Preface to *Polish Manuscripts.*

alone, he thought, the Turkish empire could be confined within bounds. He sent an embassy to the Sophy of Persia, but could not persuade him to declare war against the Porte.[1] He then tried to mediate between the Emperor and the insurgents in Hungary, and succeeded so far as to obtain a promise from Tekeli that Moravia should be left untouched.[2] Finally he tried to promote a good understanding between France and Austria, but Louis sullenly refused his mediation.

The preparations of the Grand Vizier were now complete, and in the spring he advanced his vast host to Essek, in Hungary. He had under his standards at least 300,000 combatants[3] *The Vizier's forces.* and 300 pieces of artillery. He was accompanied by Selim Gieray, the terrible Tartar khan, and by a crowd of his nomad horsemen.

The Emperor could scarcely realize the peril in which he stood. He reckoned that his frontier fortresses would detain the Turks for at least two campaigns. Fortunately Sobieski, by *Rapid advance of the Turks upon Vienna.* means of a letter which his Cossack spies intercepted[4] in Bulgaria, was enabled to assure him that Vienna would be the first point of attack. This intelligence was soon put beyond a doubt. The Duke of Lorraine, general of the Imperial forces, who with scarcely 30,000 men was covering Upper Hungary, was compelled to retreat. The whole Turkish army continued to advance by forced marches, leaving the fortresses in their rear; and Lorraine had barely time to throw 8,000 infantry into Vienna and retreat beyond the Danube, before 50,000 Tartars, the advanced guard of Mustapha, appeared at the gates (July 9). Leopold had profited by Sobieski's warning to demolish the extensive suburbs where the nobility resided, but the city was wholly unprepared for defence.

The night before Lorraine's arrival the Emperor himself with his court fled precipitately to Linz, and thence to Passau. The peasants of the southern plain were flocking into the *Panic at Vienna.* city by hundreds, while many of the citizens followed the Emperor in his flight. It was left to Lorraine, with the governor, the intrepid Count Stahremberg, to concert measures

---

[1] DALEYRAC, ch. ii. p. 44.

[2] Salvandy (ii. 161) says that in August Leopold offered to cede him the kingdom of Hungary, and to guarantee the succession to his family, and that John answered that he wished for no other reward but the glory of deserving well of God and man. The offer, if made, could not have been *bona fide.*

[3] This is the estimate of Sobieski himself in his famous letter to the queen after the battle. He bases it on the number of tents, which he places at nearly 100,000. Daleyrac says that a list was found in the Grand Vizier's tent, which gave the number of the Turks alone as 191,800.

[4] Daleyrac tells an amusing story of the way in which these Cossacks brought in their prisoners. The king offered a reward to those who could catch him a "Tongue" whom he could cross-examine. A Cossack brought a prisoner to the king's tent, flung him on the ground like a sack, and went away without a word. Shortly afterwards he came back, and putting his head into the tent, said, "John, they have paid me the money ; God restore it thee ! Good-night !"

of resistance. The fortifications were hastily repaired, and the counterscarp protected by thick palisades, but it was *Measures for defence.* doubtful whether they could stand an assault, owing to the neglect of a long security. A body of 5,000 citizens was formed to assist the garrison, which did not amount to 14,000 men. A week later (July 14) the Grand Vizier occupied the plain, and opened the trenches before the city.

Meanwhile all Europe, and especially Italy, was seized with consternation at the rapid march of the Turks. The plans of the *Terror of Europe.* King of France, who had advanced his army to the Rhine, were somewhat disconcerted. Finding himself pointed at as the cause of the invasion of Christendom,[1] he made a show of magnanimity, and suspended his threatened blow. It is even said that he offered the Emperor a contingent of 80,000 men, which was rejected with becoming scorn; but the statement seems improbable.

The Pope sent pressing messages to Sobieski to bring his succours before it was too late. The Emperor also, writing with *Sobieski urged to hasten his march.* unwonted deference, begged him to place himself at the head of the Imperial troops. "However inferior we are in number," he says, "your name alone, so terrible to the enemy, will ensure a victory." He added that his troops were waiting at Tuln, fifteen miles north-west of Vienna, and that at that point a bridge had been constructed over the Danube.[2] Lorraine, generously forgetting their old rivalry for the crown of Poland, wrote that he should be proud to serve under such an hero. His own skill had given some hope to a declining cause. Assisted by some Polish cavalry, he had captured the bridge of Presburg from Tekeli, but his force was too small to do any damage to the besiegers.

It is indeed a marvel that Vienna did not fall almost at once. Within a week of the opening of the trenches, the besiegers had *Siege of Vienna.* reached the palisade of the counterscarp, and, as cannon could not be used for its defence, many of the garrison lost their lives in a hand-to-hand combat. On the 7th of August the counterscarp was captured after an engagement in which both sides suffered great loss. The besieged especially lost many officers, and the brave governor was seriously wounded. From this time forward the city must have succumbed if the Vizier had ordered a general assault. Mustapha knew this, but he imagined that the booty would be enormous, and he did not wish it to fall into the hands of his soldiers. He had pitched his

[1] "The siege of Vienna had given terror to all Europe, and the utmost reproch to the French, who 'tis believed brought in the Turks for diversion that the French king might the more easily swallow Flanders, and pursue his unjust conquests upon the empire, while we sat unconcerned and under a deadly charm from somebody."—Evelyn's *Diary*, September 23rd, 1683.

[2] Letter of the Emperor to the King of Poland from Passau, August 24th.

vast pavilion in the gardens of the Emperor's palace, called the Favourite, and here he passed his days in the pursuit of pleasure. His miners advanced steadily, but in other respects he was inactive.

At the first news of the danger of Vienna Sobieski hastened to Cracow, where his army was assembling. His hussars answered his summons with alacrity, but the Lithuanians were slow to take the field. He had no intention of waiting for them, although the troops under his orders were scarcely half the complement of 40,000. He sorely needed funds for their equipment; but as the Papal subsidies had not arrived,[1] he gave lavishly from his private treasury. He had not intended to take his Turkish body-guard; but they begged leave to accompany him, and offered to give hostages.[2]

Measures of Sobieski.

On the 15th of August he quitted Cracow, accompanied by his son James, and having reviewed his troops at Tarnowitz, in Silesia (August 18), pushed on for the Danube. Leaving his main body at the head of 2,000 horse, he traversed like a whirlwind the plains of Moravia, and arrived at Tuln on the 2nd of September. The prince who was reported too infirm to take the field, had covered on horseback 350 miles in little more than ten days. Finding the bridge unfinished and scarcely half the Imperial forces assembled, he could not restrain his impatience. "Does the Emperor take me for an adventurer?" he exclaimed angrily. "I have left my army to command his. It is not for myself, but for him I fight." Three days later (September 5th) the Polish army under Jablonowski appeared, and soon afterwards the succours from Bavaria and Saxony.

His rapid march to the Danube.

Before the king's arrival there had been divisions of opinion among the imperial generals; now all men cheerfully obeyed his orders. The whole force amounted to 70,000 men, of whom 21,000 were from Austria, 18,000 from Poland, and 31,000 from Bavaria, Saxony, and the Circles. Of these at least 38,000 were cavalry. John had never commanded an army of nearly this strength, and he was confident of success. He bade the Imperialists consider not the vast numbers of the enemy but the incapacity of their general. "Would any of you," he asked, "have suffered the construction of this bridge within five leagues of your camp? The man cannot *fail* to be beaten."

Forces of the allies.

In his letters to the queen, which have most fortunately been preserved,[3] we can follow the inmost thoughts of the great commander during these most anxious days. He twice remarks with evident pleasure that the German troops obey him better than his own. At the same time he is

Exertions of the king.

---

[1] A grand subscription was being raised in Rome. Cardinal Barberini alone gave 20,000 florins.

[2] DALEYRAC, chap. i. p. 21, and SALVANDY.

[3] Published by N. A. Salvandy; translated by M. le Comte Plater. Paris, 1826.

disgusted with the trifling squabbles over etiquette which occupy so much of his time. Even his necessary duties allow him no leisure. "Continual harangues, my interviews with the Duke of Lorraine and the other chiefs, innumerable orders to be given, prevent me not only from writing, but from taking food and rest."[1] Yet his unreasonable consort, for whom his devoted fondness appears in almost every line,[2] complains that he does not read her letters. "I must complain of you, my dear, my incomparable Mariette. . . . Can you say seriously that I do not read your letters? The fact is that I read each of them three times at least; first, when they arrive, secondly, as I go to bed, when at last I am free, and, thirdly, when I set myself to answer them. . . . If sometimes I fail to write at length, can you not explain my haste without the help of injurious suppositions? The armies of two continents are but a few miles from each other. I must think of everything; I must provide for the smallest detail."

On the 6th of September the army crossed the Danube. The *Passage of the Danube.* splendid equipment of the king's hussars attracted universal admiration; and his ill-clad infantry looked especially mean by contrast. His officers entreated him to allow it to cross by night, but he would not consent. Whilst one of the worst regiments was passing over, "Look at this well," he cried to the spectators; "it is an invincible body which has sworn never to be clothed but with the spoils of the enemy." At these words the men, who had hung their heads in shame, marched on erect with cheerful confidence. During the crossing of the bridge a note arrived from Stahremberg with the simple words, "No more time to lose." The miners were already under the Emperor's city palace, and numbers of the garrison were dying of dysentery.

John called a council of war to decide the route which should be taken. Between him and Vienna rose the lofty ridge called the *Ascent of the Kahlemberg.* Kahlemberg; and it was necessary either to go round it by the main road, which was flanked by the Turkish cannon, or to climb direct to the summit. John chose the latter route; but it proved more difficult than he had supposed. Three days were consumed in the ascent. All the heavy baggage had to be left behind, and of the artillery only the Polish light guns could be dragged up. At length, on the evening of the 11th, the Polish hussars lighted their fires among the woods which crowned the heights, and were answered by joyful signals from the cathedral of St. Stephen. The Turks were struck with conster-

[1] SALVANDY, ii. pp. 173, 174, quoted in *Foreign Quarterly Review*, No. xiv. vol. vii.

[2] He begins every letter to her, "Seule joie de mon âme, charmante et bien-aimée Mariette!" He calls himself her faithful and devoted Celadon, and reminds her that it would soon be her turn to become the wooer. Yet he was fifty-nine years old, and she was probably forty-eight.

nation. The Grand Vizier, though he had certain intelligence
of the ascent,[1] neglected to oppose it, partly because he
Apprehension of the Turks. despised the Christian army, and partly because he
wished to take Vienna before their eyes. But he could
not inspire his troops with his own braggart assurance. During
the night John's prisoners, whom he had set free by design, came
into the camp and spread the news that the king of Poland was
commanding in person. Mustapha loudly expressed his disbelief;
but he could not prevent the spread of a panic. At break of day
he determined to lead the janissaries to a general assault, while
he detached the spahis and auxiliaries to confront the relieving
force.

From the castle of Leopoldsberg about sunset Sobieski surveyed
the scene with mixed feelings. He saw that he would have to
make his advance over most precipitous and difficult
Confidence of Sobieski. ground; but his experienced eye was not dismayed
either by the imposing array of the Turkish tents or
by the multitude of their occupants. Writing to the queen the
same night he shows his old confidence: " Humanly speaking, and
while putting all our hope in God, one must believe that a general,
who has not thought of concentrating or entrenching himself, but
is encamped as if we were a hundred miles off, is predestined to
be beaten." He complains, however, that he had not been warned
of the steepness of the descent, and must change his order of
battle. During the night the noise of the Turkish cannon was
such that " we could not close an eye," and the wind was so high
that " it seemed as if the Vizier, who is reputed a magician, had
unchained against us the powers of the air."

When day dawned on Sunday, the memorable 12th of September,
the wind fell, and the heat was most severe. John attended mass
with the Duke of Lorraine in the old church of Leo-
Advance of the allies. poldsberg, and received the sacrament. He then mounted
his horse, and ordered the advance. The right wing was
occupied by the Poles, under Jablonowski; the centre by the Ger-
mans, under the Prince of Waldeck; the left wing by
Their order of battle. the Imperial troops, under the Duke of Lorraine.[2] The
king directed the whole; but his post was in the right
wing.

The ground in their front was broken by gullies and rough
eminences, and here and there by rude parapets of earth, which
served as the boundaries of the vineyards. The Turks
Battle of Vienna. in vain attempted to defend these positions; they were
driven from point to point by the impetuous hussars,
and the Polish artillery, dexterously handled by Konski, did such

---

[1] His army probably did not know of it; but Daleyrac says he had the news from
a spy. It is inconceivable that he should not have employed a few scouts.
[2] His order of battle given in Coyer (pp. 316–318), in which the Duke of Lorraine
commanded the centre, was written previous to the ascent of the Kahlemberg.

execution that by midday the army had reached the plain. After an interval of rest the advance was continued, and the villages of Nussdorf and Heligenstadt were carried by the hussars at the lance's point, not without some loss. At five o'clock the order was given for a halt, and John proposed to rest his wearied troops before the final struggle.

Meanwhile the Vizier, who had been gallantly repulsed by the besieged, had hastened to check the retreat of the Turks. He saw with uneasiness the horse-tails on the Polish lances, and feared that after all the king might be present. At a conspicuous point in the lines he caused the hoisting of a red pavilion, which was surmounted by the standard of the Prophet, and tried to raise the spirits of his troops by his own cool assurance. Seating himself under its shade with his two sons and the Tartar khan he ordered coffee to be served.

The Polish cavalry had advanced so near that John could detect these movements with his field-glass. Provoked at this ostentatious contempt, he bade his artillerymen aim exclusively at the red pavilion, and offered fifty crowns for each successful volley. He also detached a body of hussars to seize a position from which they could fire with more effect. The cavalry dashed forward with the cry of "Sobieski for ever," and drove the Turks headlong from the spot. "By Allah," exclaimed the Tartar khan, as he heard their shouts, "the king is really among them." The Turks had also heard the dreaded name; and all at once a terrible panic arose throughout the camp.[1] "They are defeated," cried Sobieski, as he saw them waver, and ordering a general advance, he put himself at the head of the Poles with the words, "Non nobis, non nobis, Domine exercituum, sed nomini tuo da gloriam!" The shock

Rout of the Turks. of the charge was tremendous, and none but the spahis resisted it. These brave horsemen, surrounded by the rout, stood their ground, but were cut in pieces. The Vizier, weeping like a child, besought the Khan to save him. "I know the King of Poland," answered Selim; "I told you that we should have to make way before him."[2] Joining in the flight they effected their escape, although the Vizier was almost captured.

Night had now come on, and John was anxious to secure the camp in case the enemy should return. He therefore discouraged the pursuit, and forbade pillage on pain of death. He passed the night, like his soldiers, in the open air, although he took possession

The Vizier's quarters. of the Vizier's quarters. In the morning he inspected this vast bazaar of Eastern luxury, which he describes as occupying a space "as large as Warsaw or Leopol." Mustapha had come, in fact, prepared for a triumph. He is said

---

[1] SALVANDY (ii. 190) says that at this moment there was an eclipse of the moon, which increased the panic ; but Daleyrac, whose account he follows in other respects, does not mention it.

[2] Sobieski relates these particulars in Letter ix.

to have contemplated creating an empire by making himself emperor of the French. He had brought every requirement for making Vienna a Turkish arsenal, and had not omitted the materials for his mosques.' Writing to the queen on September 13th, the king says: "The Vizier has taken nothing but his horse and the clothes on his back. He has left me his heir. . . . His jewels alone are worth some thousands of ducats. . . . You cannot say to me, my heart, as the Tartar women often say to their husbands, ' You are not a man, for you have brought me no booty.' . . . The town could not have held out more than five days. The imperial palace is riddled with bullets; those immense bastions, split in pieces and half falling, look terrible."

The losses of the two armies in the action have been variously stated. Talenti, whom John sent to the Pope with what was *Losses of the two armies.* believed to be the standard of the Prophet, informed his Holiness that at least 40,000 Turks had perished.[2] Voltaire, with as little truth, states the number at 600.[3] It is evident from the letters of the king, which speak of the slain as making the neighbourhood unhealthy, that nearly 10,000 must have been slain.[4] The loss of the Poles alone was estimated at more than 1,000, and the allies probably lost in proportion.

About mid-day the king entered Vienna through the breach. He was received with acclamations. Multitudes thronged his *Entry of Sobieski into Vienna.* horse, and in spite of the frowns of their superiors openly compared him with their fugitive monarch. He entered the church of the Augustine Friars, and, as there was no priest at hand, he himself chanted the *Te Deum*. Passing on to the cathedral of St. Stephen, he remained long prostrate before the altar, while the same ceremony was performed with greater pomp. Then a discourse was preached to the assembled crowds from the text—"There was a man sent from God, whose name was John." On leaving the building, he could scarcely pass through the masses of men who pressed upon him, and begged to kiss his victorious hands. Afterwards he dined in public with Count Stahremberg, and then returned to his quarters, declaring with truth that this was the happiest day of his life.

He took an almost malicious pleasure in writing at once to inform Louis XIV. of his success. He told him that he felt it *Joy of all Europe, excepting the French king.* his particular duty to report to the most Christian king " the victory which had been gained, and the safety of Christianity." So disgusted was Louis at the collapse of his plans that he could not trust himself to answer the letter. The French civil journals, in noticing the raising

---

[1] DALBYRAC (ii. 41). This information he had from some captive Turks.
[2] He added that he had travelled for four leagues over Turkish corpses. Unfortunately for the credibility of his tale, his journey to Rome lay in the direction opposite to the field of battle.
[3] *Annales de l'Empire*. He states the Polish loss at 200.
[4] This is the number given by the French official gazette at the time.

of the siege, speak slightingly of the King of Poland, and try
to attribute all the credit to the Count of Stahremberg.[1] But no
one was deceived by these manœuvres. All Europe resounded with
the praises of Sobieski. From every Catholic pulpit he was
eulogised as the bravest defender of the Church. Filicaia and
other Italian poets sang of his glory in rapturous strains. Innocent
XI. received his envoys with the highest honours, and ordered the
standard of the Prophet to be borne in triumph throughout Italy.
Queen Christina, who was then resident at Rome, after compli-
menting the Pope, wrote Sobieski a remarkable letter, in which
she declared that she now felt for the first time the passion of
envy; she calls him emphatically the greatest king in the world,
and displays by other insinuations her hatred for Louis XIV.[2] It

Ingratitude of Leopold.
is painful to relate the conduct of the Emperor. He,
who should have been the first to thank and congratulate his deliverer, was in no hurry to meet him face to
face. Entering the city on the 14th, he contrasted with anger the
coolness of his reception with the enthusiasm shown to the King
of Poland; and it was only when he heard that John was about
to continue the pursuit that he was prevailed on to consent to the
interview. His punctilious scruples as to his demeanour towards
an elective sovereign disgusted his German allies, and the Duke of
Lorraine declared that he ought to receive the king with open
arms. At length it was agreed, on the proposition of Sobieski,
that they should meet on horseback a few paces in front of the

His interview with Sobieski.
Polish army. Let us hear the king's own account to
the queen. "I will not draw you the portrait of the
Emperor, for he is well known. He was mounted on a
bay horse of Spanish breed; he had a close coat richly embroidered,
a French hat with a clasp and white and red feathers, a belt
mounted with sapphires and diamonds, and a sword to match. We
saluted each other with politeness; I made him my compliments
in a few words of Latin; he answered in the same tongue in choice
terms. Being thus face to face I presented my son, who approached
and saluted him. The Emperor merely raised his hand to his hat;
I was astounded at it. He did the same with the senators and
generals, and even with his connection, the Palatine of Beltz.[3] To
avoid the scandal and the carping of the public, I addressed a few

[1] Yet, when shortly afterwards an official at court was presented with a sword of
Sobieski, the interest excited was intense, and engravings were taken of it.
SALVANDY (ii. 420) says that the sword of Sobieski was the cherished possession of
Napoleon at St. Helena. A French prelate was author of the witty distich :

> Dignior imperio numne Austrius ! anne Polonus !
> Odrysias acies hic fugat, ille fugit.

[2] "Votre Majesté s'est montrée digne non seulement de la couronne de Pologne,
mais de celle de l'univers. L'empire du monde vous serait dû, si le ciel l'eût reservé
à un seul potentat."

[3] Constantine Wiesnowiesçki, cousin of the late king Michael, the Emperor's
brother-in-law.

more words to the Emperor; after which I turned my horse, we saluted each other, and I rode back to the camp." John here evidently conceals as far as possible the chagrin he felt at the awkward silence of the Emperor, and his distance towards Prince James, his prospective son-in-law. Another account says that he sternly reproved a Palatine, who advanced to kiss the Emperor's foot, and that he said significantly as he turned away, " Brother, I am glad to have done you this small service."[1] After the Grand General had shown him the Polish troops, the Emperor returned to Vienna; and two days later sent a jewelled sword to Prince James, and explained that his grateful emotions had deprived him of the power of speech.

But the Emperor's ingratitude did not stop here. A day or two after the battle, the Poles (like the French after the battle of St. *Shameful* Gothard) found it difficult to obtain forage or pro-*treatment of* visions, and they were not allowed to bury even their *the Poles.* most illustrious dead in the cemeteries of the city. The king notices bitterly that, since the arrival of the Emperor, everyone shunned them as if they had the plague.[2] The Poles were furious at this studied neglect, and besought John to lead them back at once to Poland. "Our subalterns regret that we have succoured the Emperor; they wish now that the proud race had perished beyond hope of resurrection."[3]

So seldom had the army served beyond the frontiers, that its discipline, never strictly enforced, was now scarcely regarded; and numbers left the ranks and took the nearest road to their homes. John sympathised with his soldiers, but he had the ardour of a crusading hero, and he felt himself bound by his oath to pursue the infidel, and "strike a second decisive blow."[4] His letter of the 13th of September to the Marquis of Grana, shows the high *John's* hopes with which his glorious victory had inspired him. *anxiety to* He expresses his belief that the time had come for the *follow up the* collapse of the Sultan's power, and urges that further *victory.* successes in Hungary might produce revolts in the heart of his empire.[5] John has been most unjustly accused of of finding a Capua in the Vizier's tents.[6] The fact is, that during

[1] Prince Eugène, who was present, says, "N'étant pas fait encore aux manières allemandes je m'amusai beaucoup de la fière entrevue de l'empereur avec le roi de Pologne." Sa vie écrite par lui même. Paris, 1810.

[2] Letter x.

[3] Letter xii.

[4] Letter xv.

[5] "Si namque ad clangorem memoratae victoriae vel levis armorum terra marique succedat ostentatio, procul dubio gemens sub Tyrannide Grecia ac ipsa Constantinopolis perfido recalcitraret domino, suasque respiceret origines. . . . Forte Mahometanum Imperium ad sua devolvatur principia, et ubi satis in altum surrexerit lapsu graviori ruat."—Letter of Sobieski from Vizier's tent, September 13.

[6] VOLTAIRE, *Annales de l'Empire.* Curiously enough, Sobieski, in Letter x. (September 17), after mentioning Hannibal's inaction after his victory, says, "To-day we know well how to profit by ours."

the whole of the campaign, the Poles were in the van. The king was disgusted at the backwardness of the imperial court, though his high and simple nature failed to discern its motive. "It is enough to make one die a thousand times a day," he says, "to see so many opportunities slip away.[1]

The fact was that Leopold shrank from sending his victorious neighbour into a rebellious province of his empire. Yet he dared *Suspicions of* not stop him. His suspicions were increased when *the Emperor.* John received overtures from Tekeli, the Hungarian leader, and attempted to intercede for him. The Emperor's coldness had so far alienated his German allies, that the Elector of Saxony withdrew his troops, and the Elector of Bavaria threatened to do the same. He did nothing to recognise the services of the Duke of Lorraine. He coveted the spoil, and even had the assurance to suggest, through his head groom, that John should present him with some of the Vizier's horses. The gift was made and received as a due. The king also made such handsome presents to many of the German princes, that he gaily tells the queen she will have to be content with the buffaloes and camels.[2] His general distrust of the Austrians was such that he deposited his part of the spoil with the Jesuits.[3]

At length (September 17), weary of waiting for the Imperial troops, he started for the Danube. His design was to attack Lower *John ad-* Hungary, which had been a Turkish province for a *vances into* hundred and fifty years, and to invest Buda, its capital. *Hungary.* Thither the Vizier had retired to rally the remains of his army, and was avenging his defeat by the execution of a crowd of pachas. The Turks could hardly believe that the Christians would retaliate at once by invading their territory, and Sobieski's advance created the utmost alarm. But he was unhappily delayed at Presburg by a fever[4] which attacked his troops and produced such distress as to shake his resolution to proceed. *Intrigues of* Another cause of his chagrin was the scarcely-concealed *the queen.* intriguing of the queen among the troops to force him to return. She tried to persuade him that she was in constant fear of the troops of Tekeli. In two admirable letters[5] he tells her the powerful motives which induce him to continue the campaign. He shows her that the Poles are crushing their national enemy without the cost of one sou to the republic, and declares that, since the Christian armies have elected him their generalissimo, he will remain even if his countrymen desert him to finish the

---

[1] Letter x.
[2] Letter xi.
[3] Chèvremont (*L'état actuel de Pologne*, 12mo, 1702) talks of the "vile et mesquin empressement," which he showed by this act. He constantly speaks of him as "ce roi avare." As Chèvremont was secretary to the Duke of Lorraine, it is to be feared that the latter was not satisfied with his share of the spoil.
[4] A kind of dysentery, called the Hungarian fever.
[5] Letters xx. xxi.

campaign. "I have devoted my life," he says, "to the glory of God and to this holy cause, and to that I will adhere."

After a few days his troops were able to resume their march, and they were joined by the Imperialists on the 2nd of October. They crossed the second arm of the Danube, and followed its course on the left bank. The first Turkish fortress in their way was Strigonia, called by the Hungarians Gran, a place of great strength on the right bank, communicating by a bridge with the fortified suburb of Parkan on the opposite side. The vanguard of the Polish cavalry, always a march in advance of the infantry and the Imperialists, had descended the hills to reconnoitre this fort, when suddenly a large Turkish force issued from the works and appeared *He is defeated at Parkan.* in their front (October 7th.) Before the Poles could form in line they had to sustain a tremendous charge, and were put to flight. The king, who was close behind with the main body, could not rally the fugitives, and found himself obliged, with his 4,000 hussars, to charge the enemy in his turn. His onset was unsuccessful. The Turks opened their lines to enclose the Poles, and this caused a panic which ended in a rout. The king and his personal escort strove in vain to stem the rush of the Turks; they were swept along in the *mêlée.* The pursuit was hot; and the king, who was one of the last to turn his horse, was in great danger. A spahi raised his scimitar to strike him, but was hewn down before his blow fell. John was hurried along breathless, scarcely able to hold the reins, and jostled by the mad haste of his flying troops. At length the Imperialists appeared, and the Turks desisted from the pursuit. The king lay down upon a bundle of hay, sorely bruised, but more afflicted in mind than in body. It was the first defeat he had sustained, and it was embittered at first by the supposed loss of his son, who however escaped unwounded. When the Austrians came up, with sorrow in their faces and joy at their hearts, he raised himself with dignity, and said, "Gentlemen, I have been well beaten, but I will take my revenge *with* you and *for* you." His Cossack infantry, who heard that he had perished, bewailed him as a father; and he was deeply touched by their devotion.[1] Several historians have asserted that he brought on this engagement in order to crown himself with glory before the arrival of his allies; but his letter to the queen after the battle shows beyond a doubt that his cavalry had orders not to fight, and that the vanguard were taken unawares.[2]

The Poles hastily buried their dead in order to conceal their losses, and were so dispirited that the king could scarcely persuade them to wipe out the defeat. Although three days after he says

[1] Letter xvii.
[2] Letter xvi. Coyer, who had never seen this letter, takes up his favourite theme of a king pursuing selfish glory; and Coxe (*House of Austria*, ii. 449) countenances the idea.

that his body is "as black as a coal,"[1] his exertions were un-
remitting to prepare his army for a grand attack. The
Turks, as he had expected, were elated at their victory.
A report spread widely among them, which even reached
the European courts, that the hero had been slain; and they took
a fresh lease of courage. The Vizier sent them reinforcements;
and when, two days later (October 9th), the Christian army defiled
into the plain of Parkan, they found a large force drawn up to
receive them. The same morning the Turks commenced the attack,
and repeatedly charged the left wing commanded by Jablonowski.
They were beaten back with splendid courage; the steady advance of
the king with the right wing upon the fort of Parkan threw them into
confusion; and when the Christians charged in their turn, the
Turks gave way on all sides. The fort was taken by
storm, and no quarter was given;[2] numbers of fugitives
were drowned in the Danube; several pachas were
captured, and at least 40,000 Turks perished.

Great victory of Sobieski at Parkan.

Storming of the fort.

Writing to the queen on the following day, John speaks of the
victory as "even greater than that of Vienna." The Vizier was
seized with dismay, and fled precipitately to Belgrade.
His flight enabled the king to exclaim with pride that
now at last, after two hundred years of slavery,
Hungary was delivered from the infidel. He adds, "This has
surpassed my expectation, and I believe that of my contemporaries."[3]

Flight of the Vizier.

John was anxious at once to lay siege to Buda, which he regarded as the goal of the campaign, but the Duke of Lorraine
persuaded him to begin with Strigonia. This was one
of the strongest fortresses in Hungary, and had been
occupied by the Turks for a hundred and forty years.
Yet the place surrendered in a fortnight, although the garrison was
composed of 5,000 janissaries. Well might the Turkish pachas
exclaim to the Poles that their king was raised up by God to be
the scourge of Islam.[4]

Capture of Strigonia.

John could now no longer resist the eagerness of his nobles to
return to Poland. Early in November the armies separated, and
the Poles retraced their steps through Hungary. Before
their departure the king had endeavoured to mediate
between Tekeli and the commissioners of the Emperor,
but the sole favour which he could obtain for the insurgents was

Return of the Poles.

---

[1] Letter xvii.

[2] This, as Coyer says, was most discreditable to the Christians. But Sobieski
explains that the Turks had "made no prisoners" two days before, and that the
sight of the bleeding heads of Poles upon the rampart of the fort maddened his
troops.

[3] Letter xix.

[4] Letter xxi. The king notices in the same place that the Turks called him
their executioner on account of the number of men which his victories had cost
them.

the promise of a general amnesty, and his disinterested efforts only *His efforts on* resulted in increasing Leopold's suspicions of his mo-*behalf of the* tive. Yet he could not give up the attempt; he longed *Hungarians.* to establish the strong barrier of a free people against the Turkish advance; and as a last resource he begged for the help of the Holy See. In his instructions to his minister at Rome,[1] he claims this favour from the Imperial Court as his due, and indignantly disowns the unworthy motives imputed to him. "The sole interest of his Sacred Majesty is to rally the nations against the pagans. For that end he demands that the nation which he has re-conquered for Christendom should be treated after a Christian fashion." But the Pope was so closely bound to the policy of Leopold that he cared not to interfere; and nothing was done to restore the ancient liberties of Hungary. John was deeply indignant, but his conscience would not permit him to insist on this concession as the price of his sworn alliance.

His friendly relations with Tekeli were broken off by the rapine of the Lithuanians, who, on hearing of the spoils of which their *Their* tardiness had deprived them, had set off in haste *hostility to* towards the south, and were plundering Upper Hungary. *his army.* The inhabitants, regarding John as responsible for these reckless freebooters, and knowing nothing of his efforts in their behalf, shut themselves up in their towns and treated him as an enemy. Though he could scarcely obtain provisions for his troops, he was loth to relinquish his design of quartering them in Hungary. But the queen had hit on a new method of preventing him, which was more effective than the murmurs of his men. She suddenly ceased to answer his letters. "For five weeks," he complains, "I really have not known whether there is a Poland in the world."[2]

He closed the campaign gloriously on the anniversary of Kotzim (November 11th), by capturing Schetzin after a few hours' siege, *Triumphal* and then returned home through the Carpathian Moun-*entry into* tains. The ground was frozen so hard that the tents *Cracow.* could not be pitched, and it was Christmas-eve before the victorious army, laden with the spoils of the East, entered Cracow in triumph. A few days later the Grand Vizier received with resignation his sentence of death from the Sultan, and ere long the head which had dreamed of the conquest of Europe was adorning the gates of the seraglio.

The result of this grand campaign was to change the course of history. Hitherto, as at Lepanto and at St. Gothard, the Ottoman *General* arms had never received more than a temporary check; *results of the* from henceforward we find the empire of the Sultan *campaign.* constantly losing ground in Europe. John Sobieski had recovered in two months more than had been gained in a

---

[1] Quoted by SALVANDY, ii. 282-284.   [2] Letter xxix.

hundred years. The chief explanation of this decline is doubtless internal decay; but the glory of the Polish hero consists in the singleness of aim which enabled him in a moment of supreme danger to disregard old enmities, and to fly to the defence of Western Christendom, then too disunited to defend itself.

Poland gained more by this campaign than she was ready to confess. The Turks had for ever lost the offensive, and were so *Advantages to Poland.* much engaged in their conflict with the Empire, that they could not think of revenging themselves upon the republic. But they still retained the fortress of Kaminiec; and until this sore was closed, the danger seemed ever present. The Cossacks however, from whom that danger had first arisen, now acknowledged the king's authority, and falling upon the Tartars as they returned from Vienna, routed them with immense slaughter. But the renown procured by the victories of the king was more advantageous still. Venice and Muscovy besought the honour of an alliance with Poland; and she never stood higher among the nations than at this moment.

Civil troubles prevented John taking the field early the next year (1684).[1] In August, however, he marched into Podolia, and *Campaign of 1684.* after taking Jaslowicz, approached the walls of Kaminiec. Since he could not hope to reduce it by blockade, his only resource was to erect a fort in the neighbourhood; and this he effected in the face of the enemy, who dared not risk a battle.

He returned to Zolkiew in November, dissatisfied with the results of the campaign. At its outset he had been attended by *Jealousy of John's generals.* numbers of distinguished foreigners, anxious to serve under so great a prince, but he had found himself enfeebled by the lukewarm support of his two Grand Generals, Jablonowski and Sapieha. Both were jealous of his monopolising the glory by commanding in every campaign; but each of them had ulterior reasons. Jablonowski was the chief of the faction of Louis XIV., who was straining every nerve to gain over Poland; Sapieha dreamed of separating Lithuania from Poland, and becoming sovereign of the Grand Duchy. In the ensuing Diet the faction of each had its complaints against the king. The former blamed him for his ill-success against Kaminiec; the latter accused him of depriving Lithuania of her rights by summoning the Diet to meet at Warsaw instead of at Grodno. The Lithuanians at first refused to attend it, but they yielded on the king's proposal that it should be called the

---

[1] This we learn from a letter of Sobieski to the Pope, dated from Javarow, August 15th, 1684. Having 60,000 men (two-thirds of them Cossacks), he started with large hopes. "Me ad Turcarum regiam [illos] ducturum. . . . Liberator Orientis rediturus vel pro Christi fide moriturus." Sooner than give up the crusade, he announced that he would resign the crown "tamquam ut humillimus miles vitam in Hungaricis agminibus funderem."

Diet of Grodno. Their opposition to his plans, however, was relentless, and one of the family of Paz[1] carried his abuse so far as to threaten to make him feel the weight of his arm. Such was the treatment that was reserved for the saviour of Europe at the hands of his own subjects!

His health had now become so feeble that in the next campaign (1685) he was able to gratify Jablonowski by leaving him in *Unsuccessful* command. His loss was at once keenly felt. Skilful *campaign* though he was, the Grand General allowed his army to *of 1685.* be caught in a defile in the forest of Bucovina, and it required all his ability to rescue it from utter annihilation. Ashamed at his own pride no less than at his reverse he shunned the royal presence.[2]

The zeal of the king for the cause of the Emperor was cooled *Perfidy of* about this time by the marriage of the archduchess, *Leopold.* who had been promised to Prince James, to the Elector of Bavaria. The queen[3] was impelled by her resentment to join the French party, and Leopold had too much cause to fear that she would induce John to make a separate peace. He *Father Vota.* therefore sent a Jesuit named Vota as his secret agent to the court of Warsaw. The mission of the holy father was not openly political; his journey was supposed to have been undertaken to convert the heretics of the Greek church; but the Emperor trusted that his literary and social talents would procure him an ascendancy over the king of Poland. He is described as a man of wide knowledge and wonderful powers of conversation; and his religious habits and unobtrusive demeanour preserved him from suspicion. He devoted himself to the king's pleasure, and often slept on the floor of an ante-chamber in order to be at hand to entertain his weary hours. He easily kept him faithful to the league against the infidel, and hinted that the provinces of Moldavia and Wallachia might, if subdued by his arms, become hereditary in his family. John knew well that they would merely become provinces of Poland; but he was anxious *The king* to extend her frontiers to the shores of the Black Sea. *tries to revive* In spite of the opposition of the nobles he wished to *commerce.* revive her commerce; and a mercantile treaty which he contemplated with Holland would have been assisted by the acquisition of a double sea-front.

---

[1] Said to have been the same Paz with whom he fought a duel in his youth.

[2] A letter of the king to Jablonowski after this defeat, in which he gently complains of his coldness, shows his character in a most amiable light. "Whether I have merited your indifference or not, come promptly to dissipate the cloud which has covered our intimate friendship, and believe that your presence will be more efficacious towards my speedy recovery than all the art of my physicians."

[3] Chèvremont (p. 116) says that both she and the king received bribes from France, but as secretary to the Duke of Lorraine he is an Austrian authority. He admits that even on the morrow of the battle of Vienna the Emperor had no intention of fulfilling this promise of the hand of the archduchess.

By a treaty with Muscovy in this year (1686) he gave up Kiow and Smolensko, which had been long in her possession, for a large indemnity, and obtained promises of co-operation in his schemes of conquest. Posterity has blamed him for these concessions; but in his time such was the national contempt for the Muscovites that no danger was apprehended on their side.

Treaty with Muscovy.

His chances of success were excellent. The Emperor promised his aid on the side of Hungary; and a great army of Muscovites was to push forward to the Black Sea. After arranging his plans with the Imperial generals, John assembled his forces at the Dniester, but he found all alike, officers and men, indisposed to a campaign beyond the borders of Poland. But he could not now draw back. He advanced through the deserts of Moldavia to the Pruth, passing on his way the fatal spot where Zolkiewski met with a hero's death. Descending the river he entered Yassy, the capital, on the 15th of August, and found that the hospodar had fled with his troops, but had left provisions for the invading force, thinking by this means to secure his immunity from punishment, whatever might be the result of the campaign. After two days of rest John pushed on towards the Black Sea. But the heat, the scarcity of water, and the terrible solitude[1] broke the spirit of his army, and suddenly the Tartars appeared in his front. News also arrived that the Turks were within a march of him, and there was no sign either of Muscovite or Austrian succours. Leopold had again deceived him, and had profited by John's demonstration to capture the city of Buda. There was nothing left but to retreat, and this the king successfully accomplished, through a most difficult country, in the face of the enemy. The Tartars poisoned the rivers and springs, and set fire to the vegetation, while searching clouds of dust and ashes distressed the retiring Poles. At length they reached the frontiers of Poland; and the only person who had reaped any benefit from their sufferings was the Emperor Leopold.

Campaign of 1686.

In the following year a revolution at Constantinople, provoked by continued disasters, deprived Mahomet IV. of his throne; and had there been a complete accord between the members of the Christian league, the Ottoman empire might have tottered to its fall. No soldier of the Church had laboured more steadily towards this end than John Sobieski; and if it was not realised, the fault lay not with him but with his more powerful allies.

Deposition of the Sultan.

As his reign drew near its close, the internal disorders of his kingdom increased. The Emperor never ceased to intrigue with the Lithuanian grandees against his faithful ally, and the French

---

[1] The dangers of this expedition did not deter John from antiquarian researches. Passing an ancient mound he ascended it, and after examination pronounced it to be the work of Decebalus, king of Dacia.

party opposed him for this fidelity to the league. The lesser

Polish anarchy. nobility was devoted to him; but the Senate was now the hotbed of faction. All the grandees wished for the end of his reign, the French party because they disliked his policy, and the Lithuanians because they hated his person. Besides this, every ambitious senator looked to an interregnum as a means of realising his dreams of power.

In the Diet of Grodno in 1688 the king was assailed on all sides. The senators' in the pay of France clamoured for peace

Diet of Grodno. with the Porte; the Lithuanians, at a hint from the Emperor, accused him of personal aims in his attempt upon Moldavia. Before any subsidy could be voted the Diet was dissolved by the veto; and when the king assembled a convocation he met with the same stormy opposition. Hastily dismissing the assembly, he submitted to a period of inaction; but he had the consolation of finding, on a visit to Wilna in the same year, that even in the Grand Duchy he was regarded by the people with admiration.

A fresh outburst from the French party occurred in the same summer, when he refused to make peace with the Sultan, although

John refuses peace with the Turks. he was offered the restoration of Kaminiec. He had bound himself by oath never to make a separate peace without the consent of his allies; but to keep strictly to this article was detrimental to the republic, so sorely in need of reforms, and he had abundant excuse for breaking it in the conduct of the Emperor.

His scruples were not suggested by a desire for further glory, or by a blindness to the true interests of Poland. His days of war-

Tries to establish hereditary succession. fare were past for ever. He saw only too clearly the failure of the old constitution, and he was anxious before his death to witness the establishment of hereditary monarchy. In striving to have his son declared his successor he was not actuated by merely selfish motives, for when a subject he had held the same principles.[2] But the grandees considered such a proposal as a direct infringement of their privileges; and they were encouraged by Leopold, who found it his interest to preserve Poland in a state of fermentation.

The king intended to ask this of the republic at the Diet of Grodno; but his intention becoming known, he was assailed with

Affecting scene in the senate. the utmost virulence in the senate. The Grand Treasurer termed him despot, tyrant, and destructor of the public liberty; a palatine spoke of him as the enemy of his country. At length the king rose and addressed the senate. He recalled the patriotism and services of his ancestors, and protested his devotion to the cause of liberty. But he begged his hearers to

---

[1] All the orders of the realm sat together while the Diet lasted.

[2] He seems to have been in favour of John Casimir's attempt to name a successor.

pause, and reflect on the consequences of intestine strife. "Oh, what will be one day the sad surprise of posterity to see that at the summit of our glory, when the name of Poland was filling the universe, we have allowed our country to fall in ruins, to fall, alas! for ever! For myself I have now and then gained you a few battles; but I confess myself deprived of all power to save you. It only remains for me to resign, not to destiny, for I am a Christian, but to the great and mighty God, the future of my beloved country. . . . I seem to hear already resounding over our heads the cry of the prophet: 'Yet forty days, and Nineveh shall be destroyed.' Your most illustrious Dominations know that I do not believe in auguries. I do not search out oracles; I give no credence to dreams; it is not an oracle, it is faith which teaches me that the decrees of Providence cannot fail to be accomplished."

During this prophetic speech the voice of the old king trembled with emotion, and the senate was deeply touched. The primate knelt at the foot of the throne, and assured him of the loyalty of Poland; and a cry of assent arose from all present. The subsidies were voted by acclamation; but it was only a transient gleam of concord. Next year there were rumours of a conspiracy *Continued disturbances.* to dethrone the king; and amid the storms of the Diet a bishop named Opalinski said to him haughtily, " Be equitable, or cease to reign !" The insult was soon followed by an apology; but the tumult continued in the assembly, and sabres were freely used before the veto terminated the disgraceful scene.' The king felt himself unable to cope with these terrible disorders, and he instructed his chancellor to prepare an act of abdication *Intended ab- dication of Sobieski.* (1689); but the unfeigned sorrow of all classes persuaded him to withdraw it. There was little improvement, however, in the temper of future Diets; and the veto was employed as freely as before.

John was not more happy in his domestic than in his public life. His imperious queen was ever his evil genius. Not content *Discord in his family.* with diminishing his popularity by mixing too freely in public affairs,² she sowed dissension round his own fireside. The king evidently designed for his successor his eldest son James; for, besides giving him a high command in the army, he allowed him to sit by his side in the senate. But the

---

¹ Candles were not allowed in the Diet, and the session having lasted a long time, a Lithuanian took advantage of the dusk to smack a bishop in the face, and a tumult ensued. About the same time Sapieha, the Lithuanian general, had a grave quarrel with the Bishop of Wilna. One party used excommunication, and the other violence, and no efforts of the king could reconcile them.

² She was always intriguing in the Diet, and did her utmost to dissolve that of Grodno. She was accused of selling offices of state, and binding the recipient to support one of her sons at the next election (Connor). She certainly had a control over the king's appointments, and he so loved domestic peace that he generally followed her advice.

queen favoured Alexander, her second son, who was more handsome and popular[1] than his brother, and her open partiality produced a fierce hatred between the two brothers. When the Emperor,
reminded of the value of John's friendship by the victories of
Mustapha Köprili, gave the Princess of Neuberg in marriage to
Prince James[2] (1690), the queen took a violent dislike to her
daughter-in-law; and the family breach was widened.

Next year the king took the field for the last time, nominally to
chastise the Tartars for an invasion in the winter, but really
His last perhaps to escape the miseries of his court. He took
campaign, with him for the first time his son Alexander, and this
in 1691. so exasperated Prince James that he threatened to leave
the country. The king told him that if he went he would take
with him a father's curse, and he was persuaded to repent and ask
pardon for his violence. His father said openly that in the
ensuing campaign he should more easily get the better of the
enemy than of his own sons. He gained a victory at Pererita
(August 6), and took a few places in Moldavia, and then returned to
his kingdom never to leave it more.

He spent his last years in retirement, and seldom appeared in
public except in the Diet. His palace of Willanow was his
His love of favourite residence, and from thence in the summer he
retirement. would roam from castle to castle, sometimes pitching
his tent, like his nomad forefathers, wherever a pic-
turesque spot or a noble landscape attracted his fancy. The queen
would have preferred the gaieties of Warsaw; but she followed
him into his solitude, and took care that balls, operas, and the
other amusements of a court should be going on around him.

His chief recreation now, as in his most difficult campaigns,
was the study of the sciences. He complains to the queen, after
His literary the battle of Vienna, that with all his love of reading
tastes. he has not had a book in his hand for more than three
weeks.[3] When he read he always had a pencil in his
hand, and his marginal notes displayed uncommon powers of mind.
Dr. South—no mean judge—pronounces him to be "very opu-
lently stored with all polite and scholastical learning." He was
fond of writing Polish poetry, and when his daughter Theresa
married the Elector of Bavaria he presented her with a copy of
verses on the event.[4] Like many others of the Slav race, he was
an accomplished linguist. He could converse with ease in six
languages, including Latin,[5] and learnt Spanish when he was past

---

[1] Prince James (born in 1667) was called the son of the Grand Marshal, and the
other two the sons of the king.

[2] This marriage made him brother-in-law of the sovereigns of Spain, Portugal, and
Austria.

[3] Letter xi. from Presburg, September 19th.

[4] CONNOR, *Letters on Poland.*

[5] The others, besides the Slavonian, were French, Italian, German, and Turkish.

fifty. His delight was to assemble around him cultivated men like Father Vota, the French Ambassador Cardinal Polignac, and his physicians, Connor and Jonas, and to "set them very artfully by the ears"[1] on some question of philosophy or natural science.[2] Nor was theology forgotten. He used to give audiences to the schismatic bishops, and listen patiently to their arguments for their respective creeds.

Such a prince was of course an ardent patron of learning. During his reign more books issued from the Polish press than in the two centuries preceding; and his liberal views led *Patron of learning.* him to reprimand the Catholic clergy for not admitting into their schools the philosophy of Descartes. The great nobles, many of them wholly unlettered, could not sympathise with these literary tastes, and they showed their spite to-*Spite of the nobles.* wards the king in various ways. On one occasion, when illness kept him away from the Diet, the Sapiehas demanded that he should be summoned to attend; and when their motion was lost, they broke up the assembly with the veto. A Jew named Bethsal, who collected his revenues, was condemned to death by the Diet on an unproved charge of sacrilege,[3] and John could hardly prevail to save his life. Many imputed his love of retirement to covetousness, and asserted that he laid up £100,000 *Charge of covetousness unproved.* a year for the benefit of his sons.[4] The accusation has been often repeated, although his life abounds in instances of his draining his private[5] coffers to serve a pressing public need.

The disorders of the kingdom grew more frightful as John became less able to restrain them. Street brawls between political parties had always been of common occurrence, but the rioters now began to use firearms,[6] and the king had to publish an edict prohibiting the shedding of blood on pain of death. He often sent for the chief nobles, and adjured them by the love of their country to aid him in restoring order.[7] In 1695 the Tartars, tempted by Polish anarchy and by a report of the king's death, invaded Russia, and besieged Leopol; but they disappeared as quickly as they had come on the approach of Sobieski.

Reports of his death were common in Europe, partly from his feeble health and partly from the interest which many sovereigns

[1] SOUTH's *Letter to Dr Edward Pococke*, p. 5.

[2] Connor describes a discussion as to what part of the body the soul inhabits.

[3] It is to be feared, however, that Bethsal had sometimes abused his position.

[4] CONNOR, Letter iv.

[5] "The king opened his coffers to the designs of the League so far that his own family could scarcely believe it."—DALEYRAC, Preface.

[6] DALEYRAC, chap. i. p. 33.

[7] Connor says that the grandees paid him outwardly the highest respect, never eating with him at his table, and that those who most abused him in Parliament showed him great deference elsewhere.

felt in the event.[1] He had long been afflicted with dropsy;
and a wound in his head, which he had received
His feeble health. long before in the Cossack war, now caused serious
alarm.

The queen was most anxious that he should make his will, and
she deputed her Chancellor, Bishop Zaluski, to make the proposal.
The king received it with disfavour. " I am surprised,"
Schemes of the queen. he said, "that a man of your sense and worth should
thus waste your time. Can you expect anything good
of the times in which we live? Look at the inundation of vice,
the contagion of folly; and should we believe in the execution of
our last wishes? In life we command and are not obeyed. Would
it be otherwise in death?" Soon after the queen entered, and read
in the face of the bishop the failure of her plan. Zaluski tells us
that the next day the king complained bitterly to him of the bodily
sufferings brought on by a dose of mercury which she had given
him. His frame was shaken by convulsive sobs, and he exclaimed
wildly, "Will there be no one to avenge my death?" This was
probably only the raving of a distempered brain; but the queen
has never been exempt from suspicion, and her conduct after his
death only served to confirm it.

On the 17th of June, 1696, his seventy-second birthday,[2] he lay
at Willanow in a state of dreadful weakness. He asked the news
from Warsaw, and was told that multitudes were flock-
His illness, ing to the churches to pray for his recovery. The
intelligence affected him deeply, and he passed the day in cheerful
conversation; but towards evening he was seized with an attack
of apoplexy.[3] The chief officers hastened to his chamber, and when
he awoke to a short interval of consciousness he showed how eager
And death. he was to depart by pronouncing the words "Stava bene."
Soon afterwards, about sunset, he breathed his last, and
his death, like his birth, was followed by a sudden and frightful
storm.

Only a few of the nobles welcomed his decease; the mass of the
nation remembered his glory, and sincerely mourned his loss. The
Chancellor Żaluski thus expresses the general sorrow:
Sorrow of the nation. "With this Atlas has fallen, in my eyes at least (may I
prove a false prophet!), the republic itself. We seem
not so much to have lost him as to have descended with him into

[1] BURNET (*History of his Own Time*, iii. 348) asserts that "he died at last under a
general contempt." This is curious side by side with the fact that shortly before
his death the new Pope, Innocent XII., proposed to him to mediate between France
and Austria.
[2] Salvandy (ii. 395) says that it was also the day of his accession. It certainly
was not the day of his election, or of his signing the "pacta conventa," or of his
coronation.
[3] Connor says that he died of a dropsy turned into a scirrhus or hard tumour. The
blood being prevented circulating, the humours were driven to the head, and apoplexy
ensued.

the tomb. At least I have but too much cause to fear that it is all over with our power. At this news the grief is universal. In the streets men accost each other with tears, and those who do not weep are yet terrified at the fate which is in store for us. Terror apart, what grief was ever more natural ? He is, perhaps, the first king in whose reign not one drop of blood has been shed in reparation of his own wrongs. He had but one single fault—he was not immortal."

Amidst such heartfelt sorrow the behaviour of his family alienated from them all public sympathy. Prince James at first refused to admit the queen with the royal corpse to the castle of Warsaw, and when at length he yielded, he hurried away to Zolkiew to seize his father's treasures. The queen hastened after him to put in her claim, but he turned the cannon of that fortress against her. Burning with indignation, she exerted all her influence before she left the country [1] to destroy his chances of the crown. Such was the magic of his father's name that at first there was a large party in his favour; but the family quarrels weakened and dispersed it. The Austrian party elected Augustus of Saxony; and the French party thought it necessary to protest by seizing the remains of the late king. The Elector, resolved not to be out-manœuvred, erected a cenotaph to the memory of John III.; and it was not till the next reign, thirty-six years later, that his body received interment. [2]

Quarrels of his family.

The history of his three sons deserves a word of remark. Charles XII., who as a boy was a devoted admirer of John Sobieski, [3] invaded Poland in 1705, and would have offered the crown to Prince James; but the prince, being then in Germany with his brother Constantine, was seized by the Saxon troops, and honourably confined at Leipsic; and, as his brother Alexander nobly refused to profit by his misfortune, the opportunity passed by. Alexander died at Rome as a capuchin, and his two brothers resided in Poland on their estates. James Sobieski had two daughters, of whom the younger, Maria Clementina, was married to the Chevalier St. George, called the "Old Pretender," and became the mother of the unhappy Charles Edward.

His sons.

The life and exploits of John Sobieski have in modern times scarcely received their due meed of attention. Born in a country half civilized, half barbarous, whose independence has now been completely effaced, his glory has not proved so enduring as that of less remarkable men who have

Character of John Sobieski,

---

[1] It is said that she attempted to procure the election of Jablonowski with the intention of marrying him. She soon left Poland and resided in France, where she died in 1717, at the age of eighty-two.

[2] SALVANDY, ii. 409. The fact is almost incredible.

[3] It is said that he refused to learn Latin until he heard that the Polish hero was a proficient in that language. When he was told of his death he exclaimed, "So great a king ought never to have died."

figured on a more conspicuous stage. As general, as patriot, and
As general. as Christian hero, he will bear comparison with the
greatest names in any age. No man ever won so many
battles in the most desperate situations; no man ever achieved
such deeds with forces often insignificant and always unruly. His
fertility of resource was amazing; yet it was only equal to the swift-
ness of his execution. His chief glory is that, unlike any other great
conqueror, his grandest triumphs were obtained in defensive
As patriot. warfare, and that all his efforts were directed either to
the salvation of his country or to the honour of his
religion. His individual greatness appears most striking in the
ascendancy which he early acquired in his own country. His frank
and simple bearing, his noble mien, and his stirring eloquence,
enabled him, while he was still a subject, to sway the minds and
wills of his fellow-countrymen as if by an irresistible charm. He
laboured for the safety of Poland with a perfect singleness of aim;
and when that was fully secured, he strove with a like
As Christian hero. fixity of purpose for the destruction of the Ottoman
power. To us his crusading ardour may seem to have
been out of date, but we must remember that in the seventeenth
century the Turks still inspired a lively alarm, and that if at the
present day we regard them with pity or contempt, the first step
towards this change was accomplished by the sword of John
Sobieski.

As a king, he is not entitled to the same high praise. In a land
of peace and order he might have ranked as a benefactor to his
As king. people, but in the home of licence and anarchy his
temper was too gentle and refined to employ the severity
which was needed. A king of Poland, if he was to heal the
disorders of his realm, must first have made himself feared; the
natural temperament of Sobieski made him prefer to be loved.
Clemency and generous forgiveness were parts of his disposition;[1]
and the necessary result upon his policy was that he resigned himself too easily to bear the vexations which surrounded him. When
he did act, his method was most unwise; for in his principal
attempt at reform—when he aimed at establishing hereditary
succession—he exposed himself to the charge of a grasping self-
interest.

But we cannot acquit him of deplorable weakness in the manage-
ment of his own family. A hasty passion had thrown him into
As head of his family. the power of an unscrupulous and despotic woman,
and his uxorious fondness left her only too much scope
for the activity of her caprice. We have seen more
than once that he could oppose her when his duty seemed clearly
marked out for him; but, for the sake of his own peace, he allowed

---

[1] Zaluski relates several instances of his readiness to own himself in the wrong,
and of his unwillingness to avenge a personal insult.

her to intermeddle without ceasing in the affairs of Poland. The only result of his indulgence was that very misery in his domestic circle which he had sought to avoid. Of the charge against him of avarice we have already spoken. His chivalrous enthusiasm and cultivated intelligence would have gone far to disprove it, even if the treasure which he left behind him had not been found to be only moderate.

His services to his country were extraordinary, although he himself confessed that he could not arrest her fall. He found her at the opening of his career plunged in civil strife and *His great services,* beset with foreign enemies; he left her at its close with peace fully assured to her, and with her glory at its zenith. Within two years of his death the peace of Carlowitz was signed with the Turks, by which they renounced all claim to Kaminiec, Podolia, and the Ukraine. The fruit of his victories was thus fully reaped; but his efforts to revive commerce and to form an infantry among the serfs, which would have been the first step to their emancipation, were never afterwards renewed. A *Could only retard the fall of Poland.* patriot life like his may be said to have tried the institutions of his country, and to have found them wanting. After seventy-five years of anarchy, that dreaded Partition, which had been mooted in his day[1] but which he had postponed for a hundred years, was at length carried into effect. Austria, whom he had saved by his prowess, Prussia, whom he had hoped to reunite to his country, Russia, whom his ancestor[2] had laid at her feet—each took a share of the spoil. No other patriot arose to save Poland from her rapid decline; and John Sobieski may be called the last, as he was the greatest, of her independent kings.

[1] By Charles X. of Sweden. It is said that documents are in existence which prove that Louis XIV. also entertained the idea.
[2] Zolkiewski.